MW00897786

BRIGHTLEAF

BRIGHTLEAF

a novel by

RALEIGH RAND

For my family

Brightleaf

Copyright © 2013 by Raleigh Rand

Published by Raleigh Rand

This is a work of fiction. All names, characters, places and incidents are either products of the author's imagination or are used fictitiously. No reference to any real person is intended or should be inferred.

All rights reserved. Except as permitted under the U.S. Copyright Act of 1976, no part of this publication may be reproduced, distributed or transmitted in any form or by any means, or stored in a database or retrieval system, without the prior written permission of the publisher.

Paperback ISBN-13: 978-1492312451
eBook ISBN 13: 978-0-692-21292-9

Front Cover:
Lady Driving courtesy of captions.illmeyer.com.
Photo of sky with clouds by Raleigh Rand.
©Raleigh Rand

1

THE JERSEY GUY

I peek in my rearview mirror. Checking to see if he's following me again. The man with the New Jersey tag bolted to the front of his Lexus.

He is.

I know where he lives. Alone, of course, except for an ugly little poodle named Champagne. Champagne is white but has pinkish-brown stains around his nostrils, lips, and in the corners of his eyes, which I find so gross. Not that I've gotten close enough to see the pink hair; I just know it's there because I've seen this type of dog before.

I was spying on him. That's when I heard him call the dog by name. I pretended to be looking for an open house on a Sunday but was actually looking for a house with his car parked in the driveway. I had to know the kind of person I was dealing with. My window happened to be rolled down and he happened to be taking the dog out in the yard when I got a lock-down on the Jersey Guy's voice and the way he sounded when the dog didn't come to him right away. That's all I needed and kept on going.

It's been like this for I don't know how long: me leaving the house to drive the carpool, and him following me. Two out of five weekday mornings when I get to my first carpool stop, there he is, slamming on the brakes behind me, acting like I didn't put on my right blinker or use my brakes to indicate that, yes, I'm slowing down. Then he honks and swerves around me like he's driving a Trans Am in Monte Carlo.

He could be packing heat for all I know, just waiting for the right moment to tell me to make his day, like Clint Eastwood. Yesterday, when I saw him pull up to the four-way stop behind me, a block before my first pickup, I got a little panicky. I could feel him back there saying to himself, Lady, you just make my day. I dare you to slow down and pull over to the curb in front of that brick house today. I could tell he was saying that to himself, to me. Well, I showed him. I didn't stop at all. I drove straight to my second stop. He turned left at the next light, and I just kept on going. I felt I had reached a breaking point with him. The vibes were in the air. I knew that if I kept on moving, the drive-by-shooter spirit in him would subside for a while.

I've been having feelings of hate for the Jersey Guy lately. These feelings are probably wrong, but I've already tried just loving him, the way they teach in church, but I can't do it. I can't get around the fact that I hate him for making me appear like a slow-minded, white, female Southerner, with nothing better to do than listen to Dr. Kelly on the talk radio while she answers dumb questions from callers.

They say things like, Hello? Dr. Kelly? This is June. Gosh it's good to be on your show. My moral quandary is that my father, who is retired, is molesting my children. Do you think I should let him babysit anymore? I don't want to hurt his feelings.

If you've ever listened to any of the callers' questions, in only fifteen minutes you'll want to leap through the radio and smack the fool out of them. So yes, I do admit to tuning in from time to time. Just not all the time.

The Jersey Guy is an angry person. I console myself with the thought that anger is eating away at his insides, and he might die soon. I guess I shouldn't hope him to die, but if he did get really sick, that might-could be my moment to shine. I would go to his hospital room and gently tell him that I forgive him, and that I must have appeared confused concerning unspoken traffic codes all those days he ended up behind me, but believe me when I say I actually understand he has important places to get to, and that even my own cousin has a job with Corporate America so I know all about that.

We could make a connection.

He would know that I meant well and was just trying to play my part in this world, driving the carpool, and he was playing his part, going to Corporate America, and we were both actually floating down the same stream of life.

He swerves around me again, way too close to my car. I wish I'd have opened my door real quick, by accident, as he passed.

2

MAVIS

Mavis walks into the house wearing a t-shirt that would be snug on a six-year-old. We can plainly see her sixty-eight-year-old belly flopping over the top of her jean shorts. Her sagging bosoms push against the letters of her shirt, making the words *Eye Candy* look wavy, like the Scooby Doo letters.

Mavis collects t-shirts. The lady down at the back door of the Goodwill keeps her eye open for shirts she knows Mavis will appreciate; she came in here a eeks ago with a shirt reading, *I'm the BIG Sister*. Mavis's all-time favorite t-shirt comes down to her knees, so she wears it as a dress. It has an airbrushed picture of a woman's body from the neck down wearing an extra small bikini, so it looks like we're seeing Mavis herself in a bikini. The reverse of the shirt has a woman's backside, wearing a thong. I've seen this fashion before on groups of heavy-set ladies strolling Myrtle Beach, but never thought much of it until Mavis started wearing it around town in the middle of winter with a jean jacket, suntan pantyhose and sneakers.

Even though all Mavis's bottom front teeth have disappeared, and her skin shows the signs of a person who has smoked since practically a baby, with lots of teensy little lines crinkling her whole face like a wrinkled tissue, she's happy as a cricket getting those t-shirts and cooking for us.

By employing a cook, I appear elite, but actually I run a boarding house here in Brightleaf. When my grandmother passed five years ago, she left me this house on Main Street. I've lived here on and off since I was thirteen. My grandmother practically raised me. When other kids were watching MTV and *Beavis and Butthead*, I was hanging out at flea markets with my grandmother and her friends, something I resented at first but I gradually found my rhythm.

Whenever I tell people I live on Main Street, for some reason it seems like someone wearing gobs of frosted lipstick always screams, "I LOVE those old Victorian homes!"

No one around here knows their architecture, a fact I find bothersome, except the guys living in the Greek revival next door, who educated me on my particular style of home. Prairie Style is a design made popular by Frank Lloyd Wright in the early part of the twentieth century, overlapping the Victorians, which explains why you'll often see the two styles built side-by-side. But Prairie is simpler, none of that gingerbread woodwork, with a flatter roof, and clean-cut windows and doors. Frank Lloyd Wright named one of his homes Fallingwater, and in that same tradition I named my home the Rapturous Rest.

Despite its architectural celebrity, my home is known around town as a place of refuge for down-and-out folks. I've found, as far as the homeless are concerned, it's best to keep it professional, especially since my marital status is single, and since I look a little like Reese Witherspoon, it would be easy to accidentally lead them on. So I'm not *overly* friendly, but from breakfast to supper – and only in the great room – I have created a space for my boarders, the homeless or anyone else in the community to play checkers, drink coffee, chat, and watch TV without being alone during the day. Individuals who appreciate a little nod letting them know they're all right.

People need to know they're all right. Acceptance creates happiness. That's my truism. There are some who've never experienced a happy moment in their lives, people who were born into broken-down families, babies who had the misfortune of being born into totally third-rate situations. Like one minute they're safe and warm in the womb, the next minute they are pushed out into this botched operation already in progress. They can't just put on the brakes and say, *Whoa! This looks like a dark alley. Let's turn around!* If life gives them a dark alley, then they grow up in the dark.

The neighbors have nothing to worry about. I keep the lawn tidy. I also keep the heat on in the winter, the AC in the summer, the drip coffee maker in perpetual drip mode, and the TV on at all times, as a light to the weary. In that respect I'm like the Proverbs 31 woman. But instead of *her candle goeth not out by night*, it's the TV that turneth not off. I offer free meals on Wednesday nights, so naturally most people stay after for Share Group.

3

SHARE GROUP

Eleanor and I set out the chairs in a big circle in the great room. We've got two sea green sofas from the 1960s, a pair of matching paisley wingback chairs, a round oak coffee table, and a twenty-seven inch TV, but we push them all against the walls for the meeting, so everyone can have his or her own chair. I feel people are more comfortable with their own space, especially since Winslow used to like to sit too close to some of the ladies on the sofas.

Winslow looks like a shrunken head with an extra long blond ponytail and extra long legs. Put all that together, and I only want to be his friend. I know it's wrong to draw the line between romance and friendship based on whether or not a person looks like a voodoo talisman, but I can't help it. I'm inclined to believe his scary appearance runs a little deeper and implies a certain spiritual darkness. He's a psychology professor at Merritt College here in town, and a regular at our Share meetings. Even though he gives me the creeps with his tales of seducing his students, and it's apparent he wishes he could seduce me and the other females present, I let him come because he genuinely needs friends. I seriously doubt that he's seduced anyone in the past twenty-five years. Plus, how can you deny a man who cuts his own bangs and smokes wearing a jogging outfit?

Chauncey is here, too. He's done pretty well for himself, considering the way he started out in life. Chauncey's childhood trailer home kind of resembled a long, rusty dumpster. And he had a ton of relatives that lived in there with him. I heard his mother or his aunt, one, had a miscarriage. Somebody put the little dead baby in a jar of alcohol and named it Cousin It. I used to imagine them using that jar as a bookend or illuminated in a curio or something. Why is it you don't ever hear of that type thing happening in New Jersey? You'd think people from New Jersey would be crazy over an idea like a fetus bookend. Unfortunately, it happened in Brightleaf.

We are all sitting in the circle – there are seven of us this evening – and I feel I must explain the rules again before we proceed because they've been getting broken lately.

I remind everyone that the whole purpose of Share Group is to allow people to speak freely of concerns, joys, ideas and revelations without being criticized for doing so, and to offer friendly advice. Also, no laughing, snickering, or touching someone in an effort to comfort them. Everybody glances at Winslow.

We begin our sessions in silence so we can ponder before we share. To focus, I like to either close my eyes or look up at the wall, where my favorite scripture verses hang: Thou shalt neither vex a stranger nor oppress him: for ye were strangers in the land of Egypt, Exodus 22:21, and Be not forgetful to entertain strangers: for thereby some have entertained angels unawares, Hebrews 13:12. I get comfort from these because I let so many strangers come into my home, and one might even be an angel. An angel could be cleverly disguised as a house painter, like Jimmy over there.

Everyone is silent.

Finally, Jimmy clears his throat and speaks, "Lately, I've been mixing cough syrup with valerian to get high."

Silence.

"I highly recommend it."

"Cool," says Ned.

"So how much cough syrup and valerian do you use in this formula of yours?" asks Eleanor.

"Depends on your mood," says Jimmy. "Heck, cough syrup on its own is pretty awesome."

"Have you asked a doctor about that?" asks Eleanor.

"A doctor?" Jimmy looks at Eleanor like she's five. "Why would I do that?"

"For safety reasons."

Jimmy laughs. "If I told a doctor I was using cough syrup and herbs to get a big buzz, he would be all like—" (Jimmy changes his voice to sound real educated) "—Mr. Riddle, cough syrup should only be used for the purposes on the label. I cannot recommend you use it for recreation."

Everybody laughs at this. And then Jimmy says, "But you know the first thing that doctor is gonna do when he gets off work is drive straight to the closest Super Wal-Mart and buy some Robitussin and valerian. I need to pay a doctor for advice like I need to buy a wagon wheel."

"Sounds scary," I say.

Vanessa says, "You get all that at a Wal-Mart?"

Jimmy says, "Mainly the Internet. I'm in my kitchen like a mad scientist, mixing and experimenting. Substituting ashwagandha for passion flower, feverfew with balm of Gilead."

"Interesting," I say.

He says, "I'm serious, I can fix whatever ails you. Next time you get pink eye or ringworm, call me and I'll fix you up."

Several people mumble to their neighbors until Ned, my carriage house boarder, speaks up.

"Just thought I'd say that I agree with Jimmy. I never really try to mix my own medicine, but don't go to doctors, either. Too expensive, man. And I'm always a little paranoid that some doctor is going to try a secret experiment on me. You know, like give me a placebo when I really need an antibiotic, just to see if I'll die."

Mavis says, "Doctors don't try and kill folks."

"You never know, man," says Ned. "Don't forget MK Ultra." Jimmy points his finger at Ned, like he just hit the nail on the head. Then Ned says, "Hey, not to change the subject or anything, but I had a kick-ass dream last night. Wanna hear it?"

We all nod because that's what we do at Share Group.

"Okay, The Three Tenors," says Ned. "Remember those dudes? And that dude Pavarotti? The one with that wicked beard? Dude looks like a villain, man!"

Jimmy and Winslow start laughing.

"Lots of people have wicked beards," says Winslow. "Abraham Lincoln, ZZ Top, Colonel Sanders."

Ned nods, "Hey man, don't get me started on the Colonel. Anyway, those dudes were planning this new show. It was gonna be like a reality show about people who can sing opera super good and perform impossible tasks at the same time, like beat Pac Man and eat six saltine crackers in one minute.

"At first those Tenor guys had trouble deciding between me and the little kid from Malcolm in the Middle. I should have been scared shitless, but since my dreaming self knew the real me watched all the Malcolm shows, the dreaming self had an amazing amount of confidence. Anyways, Dewey was trying to sing, run a three-legged race, and balance a checkbook, but I was teaching quantum physics in a WWE Smack Down ring, and keeping perfect pitch."

"Stop," says Winslow. "We don't want to hear this whole dream. Dreams are only for the dreamer. And who is Dewey?"

Ned stops and looks at Winslow. Like he feels sorry for him.

Ned says, "You don't know Dewey?"

Winslow shrugs.

Ned says, "I'm almost done. Listen, my fake wrestling was sick! And then I did the worm. Dewey tried to do the worm but couldn't. He'd gotten a little older, and kinda soft around the middle, so he wasn't as powerful."

"You da man!" shouts Chauncey.

Ned stands up and gives Chauncey a high-five across the circle. "Yeah man, it was sweet."

Eleanor asks, "What exactly is the worm?"

Eleanor has a thing for Ned. He's cute, if you're into bohemian types. He's got an innocent quality, something that Eleanor loves in men. Someone she can mother and control.

Ned is still lovin' on the memory of that dream. His shoulder-length hair is tucked behind his ears. He says, "The worm is a breakdance move. It's been around forever."

"Can you really do it?"

"I can."

Chauncey says, "The worm is easy."

Ned gets excited and claps his hands together and says, "It is! Show them, man!"

It is apparent Chauncey gets nervous doing the worm in front of people. Or else he suddenly can't remember how to do the worm because he says, "I can do it. My three-year-old nephew can do the worm, and my sister is super at it."

"Smokin' family!" says Ned.

"But I don't feel like getting all dirty," adds Chauncey, smoothing his pants.

"This floor ain't dirty," says Mavis. "Vanessa mopped it not three hours ago."

Vanessa says, "Go 'head, and eat some ham off this floor. Clean as Clorox."

I say, "Come on, Chauncey. Show us."

Chauncey finally confesses to not having performed the worm in a while, and he's worried about pulling a muscle in his back, but he wouldn't mind seeing Winslow eat ham off the floor.

"I'll lick peanut butter off the floor if Ned will show us the worm," says Winslow.

All of us, sitting in the circle, draining our coffee cups, beg Ned to show us the worm.

Ned begins to blush and shake his head, but you can tell he's making a decision, and picturing himself breakdancing in front of seven or eight people.

Then Ned stands up, pushes back his chair, rolls up his sleeves, and sort of throws himself onto the ground and begins to make his body go in a wave-like motion. His hair swishes back and forth across his cheeks to the rhythm of his rolling movements. Right there in the center of the circle. You would never imagine Ned could do this type of thing that demands a certain amount of physical strength. Muscles even. I always thought Ned was your basic video game stoner, but it's apparent he works on his worm skills with frequency.

Ned stands up, does a quick bow and tucks his hair back behind his ears and says, "That's how it's done, man."

Everyone claps. I can tell Ned is pleased, and he will walk away from this night with new confidence, and everyone here will remember this moment.

Winslow starts to speak. I forget where he says he's from, but I always think Minnesota. And he talks real slow, like he's trying to be smooth. Since he's a psychologist, he sometimes tries to help people in the group with professional comments.

"Ned, dreams can help us realize our potential. It's good you remembered that dream because we often forget them, and the purpose is lost. Start keeping a dream journal. It will help you understand yourself better."

"Will do," says Ned.

We all sit there, wondering if anybody is going next, because some nights I can't get people to shut up so we can all go home. But everyone just sits, like they're waiting for the next act. Or maybe they're thinking they might make a quick stop at Super Wal-Mart on the way home. Since everyone seems so introspective, I decide to go ahead and say what I've been meaning to share. It's nothing big, but I've been thinking about it all day.

"Dr. Kelly is encouraging all women, via radio, to go to the gynecologist and get a mammogram," I say. "And if you send her a copy of your results she'll send you a free t-shirt that says, This Mama Got Her Mammo."

The men shift in their seats and stare at the floor. But that got Mavis's attention all right. Besides getting a shirt, she loves going to the gynecologist. Eleanor rolls her eyes because she's skinny as a moray eel and has no boobs. I, on the other hand, am putting on the brave face of a leader because I do have something going on. I've never had a mammogram, and I'm terrified.

4

THE GROCERY PALACE

The grocery store is a haven for me. I love it the way some people love a park, a museum, or Home Depot. I cruise down cool, waxed, vinyl floors in solitude, absorbing the various canned goods, labels, and produce and listening to The Grocery Palace's own music station piping in a jazzy rendition of *Stayin' Alive.*

I'm on friendly terms with the deli girl. We chat regularly while she slices the meats and cheeses, wearing her hairnet. We talk about the weather, the price of gas, and fret over people with earrings in their tongues (like, what do they do when they get a glob of alfalfa sprouts all tangled around it? Or hairs matted into it?). I also enjoy chatting with the boy at the seafood counter and the cashier about the goings-on around town. The seafood boy has a tattoo of a flaming grim reaper on his neck and should trim his nose hairs with more regularity, but he's a good conversationalist and is relatively knowledgeable about salmon.

The cashier will sometimes tell me things I do not wish to know. Such as who has bounced checks lately or purchased pregnancy tests. Since The Grocery Palace (or the G.P., for short) is privately owned, it tends to be more intimate than the big chains, which I love, but it can sometimes verge on too intimate. I make a mental note not to purchase personal items when that cashier is working, otherwise the whole town will know when Mary Beth Green has personal afflictions whether they want to or not. I can hear that cashier now, "Well, hey there. What a fine sunny day it is, but poor Mary Beth Green is not enjoying it as we are. Her acid reflux is flaring up big-time. I told her she had no business buying that chocolate bar the other day." But normally we have pleasant conversations about my tomato plants or the grand opening of a new cafeteria or did we see that full moon last night and stuff.

Sometimes I come to the G.P. when I'm down in the dumps, even when I don't need groceries, because everyone here is friendly. The employees and patrons alike give one another a smile and the benefit of the doubt. The climate is always controlled, the music always mellow. No pushing, foul smells or loud noises. It's the way the world was meant to be beyond those sliding glass doors—peaceful, abundant, and kind.

I'm in my own world as I stock up on food. I feel like a benevolent queen buying good things for my people. Mavis normally helps me shop, but she's having a tooth pulled today. So I'm on my own, and that's just fine with me. I'm about to turn down the paper products aisle when I see a vaguely familiar form looking at the napkins. I freeze. My smile stops smiling. Jesus, help. I want to avoid the Jersey Guy at all costs. No telling what kind of commotion he'll stir up if he sees me. He looks up and slowly turns my way, as if he feels my presence. In a flash I make a U-turn down the cereal and coffee aisle and push my cart to the back of the store. I park it in front of the meat counter and tell the butcher I'll be back as I run to the restroom. The butcher nods; he thinks I'm gonna pee my pants. I swing through the restroom door and stop in front of the mirror. I'll wait here until the Jersey Guy leaves the store.

The restroom mirror is unkind today. My forehead is crevassed, and my body language is all inward, with crossed arms and hunched shoulders, like the woman who used to work at the 7-Eleven in Chapel Hill that I was always feeling sorry for. I massage the space between my eyes with my fingertips and say, "I'm not going to leave this bathroom until the Jersey Guy is gone from The Grocery Palace. What could he be buying? He's already gotten his napkins, so now he's probably moved over to the coffee aisle. He remembers he likes cream with his coffee, so now he walks to dairy. Walking, walking, walking to dairy. Picking up half and half. He also likes sugar in his coffee. It will take him a while to remember that sugar is with baking goods and not back in the coffee aisle. Walking, walking past cake mixes and flour and spices to sugar."

I go on this way for a decent amount of time, walking the Jersey Guy all over the store in my mind and out loud, searching out bread, cheese, olives, mayonnaise, roast beef, and ice cream sandwiches. When I feel a sufficient amount of time has passed for a single man (or a family of eight) to find the things he's come for, I peek out the restroom door. At that same time I hear a toilet flush behind me. Somebody has been sitting in a stall listening to my every word. Hopefully whoever it is couldn't see my feet and identify me by my shoes.

I grab my cart and try to blend in with the other shoppers heading down the paper products aisle. It looks like the coast is clear. I start feeling comfortable again. I walk to the frozen goods section and pull stuff out of the deep freeze: bags of green beans, okra and corn, Salisbury steaks, Italian bread with the garlic butter already spread on it, and three frozen lasagnas. I smile at the seafood boy with the jungle of nostril hairs, and he smiles back. I take deep breaths in and out through my nose and move boldly to the produce section for lemons. I feel my forehead loosen and my shoulders relax and I sway my head from side to side to release tension in my neck. My breathing is easier now, and I to return to my shopping with a paced normalcy.

My shopping is finished. I regard my cart with a certain peace that comes from creating a meal for the purposes of charity. I've got all the frozen stuff, ten cans of baby peas, a jumbo pack of Lipton tea bags, two heads of lettuce, a pound of sugar, a big box of instant mashed potatoes, three Sarah Lee coffee cakes, twelve lemons, a jumbo pack of paper towels, and a package of razors.

I smile and feel kindness sweep through me as I pull up to the checkout. I glance at the *People Magazine* (the thinking woman's *National Enquirer*) and wonder what the celebrities are doing these days. Sometimes I like to think of one celebrity and try to imagine what she is doing at this exact moment. Something regular, like making coffee or brushing her teeth. Thoughts like this help me avoid being impressed by the rich and famous. We're all doing the same things, except we can't all be famous.

I've reached the cashier, but now I can't find my razor coupon. It's a good one, too; razors are seriously expensive. It makes me ill that some sicko is getting filthy rich off the reality of body hair. Hair is a funny thing, wanted in certain places and taboo in others. For instance, if a man grows hair on his chest, lots of people think it's great, but if he grows it on his shoulders, it's weird. And people look at that hairy-shouldered man like he chose to put it there. He is judged by where hairs chose to locate themselves on his body. And when women have unwanted hair...where is hair wanted but on their heads? But see, if there's this woman with a mustache and a hairy back, people look at her like she willed the hair to grow there. In our minds, we know she's an unwilling vessel, but most people can't help but think the opposite, like *deep in her heart she has a mustache*, like she's mustache to the core. I might start boycotting the high price of razors—but then I'd have to move to Germany. One summer my grandmother hosted some foreign exchange students from Germany. The hairiest girls you ever set eyes on.

I better find that coupon.

I check my wallet, purse, and pockets. Even though I'm holding up the line of people behind me, I'm fine with it because I come to this store all the time, and this might be the second time in history I've held up a line. I turn my pocketbook upside down on the counter and sort through coupons, receipts, and pennies stuck to ancient pieces of candy.

After a minute or so, a voice speaks to me from the back of the line. The voice is slightly irritated. "Whaddya need? Dime? Penny?"

I turn around and there he is. He's taller up close. The day I passed him taking out his dog I got the impression he was a little wider, too, but maybe that was just his jacket. But here he is, looking less like Danny DeVito and a little more like Andy Garcia. He looks at me over his glasses like he expects an answer. What's he doing here? Behind me? He's in my face like one of those old computer pop-up ads reminding me to speed up my performance: in need of an upgrade. I look in his cart and see far less than I have in mine. What took him so long to pick up napkins, dog food, bottled water and Fanta orange drink? Maybe he got sucked into a long conversation with the deli girl. Or took a nap in the soft drink aisle. Also, why can't I end up behind him some day? Why can't I be the one feigning impatience, telling the world how I'm too important to be suffering behind someone like him?

"She's looking for a coupon," says the cashier.

"A coupon? For how much?" Then I hear him quietly say, "I've gotta meeting to make. I'd give her a dollar to quit looking for that coupon."

Several people behind me snicker. I look at the cashier and roll my eyes. She knows me well, and nobody knows the Jersey Guy from Adam. We could easily gang up on him and stuff him in the trunk of his car. But I should deal with this on my own, so I turn around and look at him standing at the back of the line.

I casually say, "Well, if this isn't déjà vu."

Everyone in line turns to look at him too.

"Do I know you?" he asks.

Now everyone turns to look at me. And one woman is staring at my shoes.

I open my mouth to say something. But then I look at the cashier and the others in line. They are giving me this look like, *Well, does he know you?*

You can plainly see how this looks to everyone, like I'm that type of person who approaches strangers and starts talking real personal to them, like I'm suffering from some form of social illness. But this man, he does know me.

"I'm sorry," I say in my quietest voice. "I must have mistaken you for someone else." Then I get out my wallet while shaking my head, like old people do with rude teenagers, to passively communicate how their parents neglected to teach them anything of value.

I pay for my groceries without finding the coupon, smile at everyone all around like I am perfectly fine, nod at the cashier and push my cart towards the sliding doors.

It appears that the Jersey Guy is the new darling of The Grocery Palace.

Outside, drops of rain land on my hair and trickle through to my scalp. I slowly push my cart across the parking lot to my Subaru, disoriented, feeling like a stranger in my own town. This Jersey Guy, this demolition derby wannabe, has caused me to lose face on my own territory.

This is war. There will be no bedside vigils.

On New Jersey in General

I'd just like to make a comment about New Jersey. I don't know anyone from New Jersey personally, but I can tell it's a state full of line-breakers. Yankee line-cutters are in full form at the DMV. Sometimes they're crippled Yankees though. Like, "Feel sorry for me because I'm crippled, so I'm getting in front of you." Of course we Southerners feel sorry for them, and we'd gladly pave the way to the front of the line for them, if they'd be polite. Then there are the ones who break in line by pretending they don't see you. Sometimes they do it while talking on the cell phone so they can pretend even more they don't see you. These are people who would take the last biscuit at supper.

5

FLOYD

It's 9:05 a.m., and I've just dropped off the carpool at Toddlers Are People, Too. Also known as TAPT. My friend Shirley owns TAPT and mentioned some of the single mothers could use some help getting their kids to school. It seems funny to a lot of people that I drive those kids around but I enjoy it. God only knows those single mothers could use a break.

It's a glorious day. The sun is shining through the huge oaks in town, stamping flecks of light on lawns and sidewalks. The leaves are slowly turning from green to yellow and orange, and the smell of curing tobacco hangs in the air. The Jersey Guy should be well on his way to Corporate America, if not already there. I park about a block from his house and take a leisurely stroll up the street with a dog biscuit in hand. I am in a righteous mood. I consider my actions at this moment a mission of mercy, which I have dubbed *Operation Pink Stuff*. I have come to understand, after hours of wrestling with the idea, that Champagne could *very well* be in harm's way. I mean, what if this dog is in danger? You see the kind of owner he has. The Jersey Guy is practically a maniac. I am a dog social worker at this moment, moving fearlessly to rescue a minor in distress and place him in a loving home, out of the grasp of a very bad man. I slow my pace as I approach the Jersey Guy's house.

You can learn a lot about a person based on his front yard. If a yard is unkempt and strewn with broken toys, it alerts you right away that the owner is inside this very minute slurping down tallboys, watching a *Judge Judy* marathon. Secondly, I've found people who plant fake flowers around their mailboxes believe they are fooling everyone. Finally, if a person has more than one gazing ball and wind chimes galore, it's a verifiable fact that either an English professor or a pagan lives there.

The Jersey Guy's yard was more normal than I'd have thought. I'd pictured him as a statuary person: someone with a menagerie of mythical woodland creatures peeking out from behind trees and popping up between ferns, mainly because the statuary people tend to be the most emotional and unreasonable. I was wrong though. The Jersey Guy has no statuary to speak of. His yard is mown and tidy. Even an edger is employed.

He's also got a fenced-in backyard. There's no underlying significance to a fence around a backyard. A fence is normal, and has never factored into a person's character, as far as my criteria are concerned, except I figure that must be where he keeps the dog.

Champagne is right there behind the fence, barking his little nasty pink mouth off. I'm glad I don't need to break any windows because that would constitute breaking and entering, common burglary, which is something I could never do. This should be easy as pie.

I say in my sweetest voice, "Now, Champagne, it's all right." I hold the dog biscuit close to the chain link fence. "It's just me, Mary Beth. I'm a friend of your daddy's."

Champagne slows his barking and backs away from my hand. He whimpers a little, barks one more time, and moves forward some, sniffing out the treat. He begins to alternate between low growls and high-pitched whimpers. He knows he should be mean, but he wants this doggie biscuit real bad. "Champagne, you are a terrible watchdog," I say in a soothing tone, like I'm telling him he's good. I slowly reach my hand through the gate and lift the latch from the inside. The only kind of accosting Champagne knows how to do is sniff and lick my hand while I lead him out of his yard.

We are home free from here. He has no problem following the scent of the biscuit all the way to my car. I feel just like the Child Catcher from *Chitty Chitty Bang Bang*, tiptoeing around my car saying in a singsong voice, with my best Vulgarian accent, "Come little doggie, come get treats! Puppy Chow! Squeaky toys!" He hesitates a second, looks at the biscuit in my hand, hops right in the car, and gobbles it up. The Jersey Guy will never see this dog again.

"The first thing we've got to do is give you a new name," I tell Champagne, glancing at him in my rearview mirror. "How 'bout Pink Eye?"

Champagne looks at my reflection in the mirror and cocks his head. He knows I'm talking to him. "Or Conjunctivitis. Junk for short."

I chuckle to myself, thinking what a good name Junk would be for a dog. People will laugh and say they get it. Just like the junkyard dog in "Bad, Bad Leroy Brown."

Then I look in the rearview again and see this dog sitting on the backseat. He believed me when I said I was a friend of his daddy's. I realize it would be mean to call that dog Junk, and wonder how I came to be so heartless. "That'd be about as rotten as calling you Champagne," I tell him.

I get another idea. "How about Pink Stuff? Or Pinky?" I steal another glance at him in the mirror and can tell that he isn't a Pinky. "Too sissy, huh? I know what you're thinking; Pinky is about as girlie as Champagne."

I drive along wracking my brain for variations of pink. Fuchsia. Rose. Coral. Salmon. I flip on the radio. Pretty soon I catch myself humming along to an old Cranberries song. Cranberries make me think of a bladder infection. After that, a Billy Joel song comes on and I start thinking how I've always thought Billy Joel was an ugly man, so it's very good he's got singing going for him. Then another old song starts playing: *Leave those kids alone.* The fact that Pink Floyd comes on the radio at this very moment tells me that the Lord is with me. This is Divine Providence if I've ever heard it.

"How would you like me to call you Pink Floyd?" I ask the dog in the backseat. As if finally I've thought of the finest name a dog could want. The dog plants his paws on the door handle and presses his nose against the window, so I push the window control on my door panel and roll his down. He sticks his whole head out.

"How about Pink Floyd?" I call back to him. But he just sniffs the air like it's sweeter than sirloin. "I guess we can take out the Pink part," I say. "Plain old Floyd? I had a grandfather named Floyd. It's a family name and fairly manly." The dog's ears are flapping in the breeze, his tongue is hanging out, and it looks like he's smiling. I take that as a yes.

The newly christened Floyd is sitting in the great room of my house. He has already scampered around the whole downstairs, sniffing and whimpering, clacking his little toenails all over my hardwood floors. He has finally given up trying to find something that smells familiar or edible and decides to sit and rest a minute.

I pull out the phone book and sit on the sofa with my cell phone, preparing to make a few calls when Eleanor walks in the house with her arms full of shopping bags from Williams-Sonoma and Nordstrom.

I say to her, "I thought you already spent up all that money."

"Nooo!" She smiles and tries to give me a confident look that says, *I have lots of money left over from my trust fund, seeing I spend no money on food because I live on laxatives, iceberg lettuce, and coffee. And I save money by renting the room in your boarding house, thus making a sacrifice in my quality of life so that I can help you reach out to all the poor, lost, hurting souls out there.*

At least I assume that's what she's thinking.

Eleanor's way of helping people is buying them goods that they could never afford otherwise. It's not like she's going out and buying Cadillacs for listless crackheads or anything, but if I see her give another homeless person a blender (so they can make smoothies) or a shoeless person a vacuum, I might just have to take her down. Nevertheless, I find myself unable to speak to her on the subject, seeing that it makes her happy, especially since she's attracted an adoring fan base over at the homeless shelter. But her giving isn't always innocent. She's aware that she makes people feel beholden to her.

"Maaavis!" Eleanor screams, like Mavis is her own personal servant. "Come see what I bought. Help me get these bags up to my room. Cute dog. MAVIS!"

"I'm sorry!" shouts Mavis from the kitchen. "But Eleanor babe, I'm working on somethin right now."

Mavis is probably feeling guilty for saying no because this very moment her bed is draped in a new down comforter, courtesy of Eleanor. Eleanor rolls her eyes and stomps upstairs, carrying her own bags.

I've got calls to make, so I ignore Eleanor's unChrist-like behavior.

"Hello?" says a man's voice. "Peticures Doggie Stylists. How may we help you today?"

"Yes," I say, "Do you dye dogs?"

"Dye? No, ma'am, we only do highlights."

"Do you know anyone who does dye dogs?"

"I can't say there's much of a demand for it here in Brightleaf, but you'll probably find some groomers in Greensboro who can help you. If the dog has a graying problem, you could always try Miss Clairol or Lovin' Care, and wash that gray right out."

"Okay. Thanks," I say, and set the phone down.

I look at Floyd. "Miss Clairol, huh?"

"Did I hear Eleanor say, *cute dog*?" Mavis is looking through the kitchen door at Floyd curled up at my feet. He has switched positions at least ten times in the last fifteen minutes.

"Hey there, baby, where'd you come from?"

Floyd lifts his head and whimpers. He can spot a softy.

So can I.

I seize the opportunity and say, "Mavis, you will not believe what all I've been through this morning. I rescued this dog from an abusive owner. See, I spotted the owner kicking it at the park on my way to the preschool. You can imagine the horror I felt and prayed that somehow I could find a way to help this poor creature. Lo and behold, on my way back I noticed the dog making a run for it. I simply slowed down the car, leaned over, and swung open the passenger door and said, *Hop in, my man* to Floyd here, and he jumped in and we were off."

"Floyd? That's his name?"

"Well, yes, I took the liberty... Mavis, I need your help. His owner may come around searching for him, so we need to disguise him." I pause and then add for good measure, "The man looked like a real pervert, too."

Mavis nods with gravity in the same way she would if we were protecting a battered woman. "Know just what to do. A few boxes of Rit Dye should fix him. Here, give him to me and rest assured," says Mavis.

"Rit Dye?" I ask, kind of dubious. "Isn't that stuff for dyeing old blue jeans?"

"I swear by it. Rit's good for anythang needin a little pick-me-up," she says. "Take a box of red. You're fixin to go to a party and only have you an old blue dress, right? Drop that blue dress in a bucket of hot water with a red packet, pull it out an hour later, and you got you a new purple dress. Then dip your little fanger in the bucket of red and rub it on your cheeks and lips, and baby, you got yourself some make-up won't come off, no matter how drunk you get, how hard you cry, or even if you get locked outside and have to sleep in the bushes. You wake up from that night and look like a thousand dollars."

"Is this your personal experience?"

"I ain't done that in years, darlin. Anyway, I got a question," says Mavis.

"What?"

"How bout a small tattoo?"

"Tattoo?"

"You know, for Floyd here."

"That might be considered animal cruelty."

"Not a real one. I mean one of them fake tattoos. The rub-on kind."

"Whatever."

"Oh, goody," says Mavis, clapping her hands. "Come on now, Floyd baby."

She may have some strange ideas, but I love that woman. Okay now, I just have one more call to make that I've been avoiding.

"Hello. Gentle Care for Gentlewomen," answers a woman's voice.

"Hi, I need to make an appointment for a mammogram. No, I've never had one. A what? No. I guess I should do that, too, then. I prefer a woman doctor. Is that possible? Mary Beth Green. Ten a.m. on Tuesday? Thanks so much."

I have to hand it to Mavis for doing such a professional job on Floyd. Even though the color she used was Midnight Black he turned out more of a deep blue, which is quite attractive. Mavis was worried that if she used more dye she might blind Floyd, or give him brain damage. On Floyd's shoulder is a little shaved patch plastered with a rose tattoo. The dog looks ready to jump on a Harley and ride down to Daytona.

"Floyd could use a leather jacket," I say.

Floyd's been with us for three days now and is stinking up the whole downstairs. Mavis says that's because he's been eating like a horse but is too nervous to relax his bowels. I think he's traumatized after his rescue and being in a strange house, not to mention getting a new hairdo. I need to think of a way to help him relax. All he really needs is a familiar setting to do his business.

The Jersey Guy should be at work while Floyd has a rendezvous with his old yard. I rub Floyd's little curly head and tell him it's gonna be all right and carry him out to the car. We ride with the windows down so Floyd's gas won't kill us both. As we approach Floyd's old neighborhood, it's apparent he knows exactly where he is. As soon as he catches a whiff of it, he jumps up with his paws on the back window and whimpers like dogs do when they're riding in a car and get close to an old stomping ground. When I open the door, he bolts down the street to the Jersey Guy's yard but cannot make it to the grass, so begins to make his debut as Floyd the Dark Blue right there on the driveway.

Floyd takes his time, too. Even though I've been standing here waiting for him for maybe thirty seconds, it feels like he's been hunched over forever.

Hurry up, Floyd. I'm antsy to get us back in the car. Then out of the blue I hear this buzzing sound. It is the buzzing sound associated with electric garage doors. The Jersey Guy's garage door begins to slowly creak upwards. I start to panic. An ignition starts, and the rear end of his Lexus begins to appear under the rising door. Floyd is not quite finished.

"Floyd. Come. Come here now! Hurry!"

Floyd is not coming.

"Floyd, come!" I whisper as loud as I can. "Champagne!"

He has finished the deed, but won't come. He just looks at me, like he's deciding. Weighing his options. Should he stay here with the Jersey Guy, or should he go with his kidnapper? When the Jersey Guy sees his dog has been dyed blue, he'll call the cops, and it will be all over the *Brightleaf Daily News* that someone vandalized the Jersey Guy's dog. Me and Mavis will go to jail. Mavis will be cleared, and I alone will rot in prison forever.

The garage door is all the way open. I turn and start sprinting towards my car. I am busting my butt to get my keys out. My hands are shaking, and my brain is in full throttle freak-out mode. I pull out my sunglasses, shoving them on my face, keeping my head turned away from the scene unfolding behind me.

The Lexus begins to back out of the garage. I can't look. I won't watch. I reach my car and open the door and am shocked when Floyd hops up onto the front seat. I turn to look back at the Jersey Guy's house. His car has backed out all the way onto the street, with one long brown tire mark going down the driveway. Then the Jersey Guy drives away.

Floyd looks at me expectantly, panting, his tongue lolling out, with a huge grin on his face. He knows he was playing me back there. I pull a dog biscuit from the glove compartment and hand it to him, my heart still beating through my eardrums, and say, "You did good, Floyd."

6

THE GYNECOLOGIST

I stand in my bedroom, wearing only my bra and underwear, debating what to wear to my doctor's appointment today. I decide against a dress because when they ask me to take off my shirt for the mammogram, I'll have to take off the entire thing. So I opt for a shirt that buttons up the front and a skirt, just in case.

I am paranoid of hidden cameras. I don't really believe that a female doctor would have hidden cameras for depraved reasons like a man doctor might, but mainly to catch women stealing stuff, like alcohol prep pads. Those are handy. I think women in general just like to snoop—to open drawers real quietly, look inside and close them again. My own curiosity is kept in check by the fear that there are probably hidden cameras everywhere.

I read on the Internet once that a lawyer had hidden cameras planted in the toilets at his office. *Recording from inside the toilet.* I wondered what he did with those videos. Like come home from a long day in court, microwave a Lean Cuisine, loosen his tie, and relax on the sofa to one of those videos? A good rule of thumb would be to inspect a lawyer's toilet really closely before you hire him.

I'm in the waiting room of the Gentle Care for Gentlewomen office. I spend twenty-five minutes filling out the required paperwork, then pass it back to the receptionist. The name of this place cracks me up. I admit, the Gentlewomen part initially drew me in, but it still strikes me as strange because I know a lot of women who are seriously not gentle. Women who could put a flying monkey in a full nelson. Where do those gals go for OB/GYN? Nurse Ratched?

The walls are painted a soothing mint green and hung with framed photos of waterfalls and gurgling brooks. I'm aware the photos and the color scheme are all about promoting a feeling of peace and safety. It works for me. I pick up a *Town and Country*, immediately flipping to the pages where they show all the filthy rich brides and grooms whose parents threw them multi-million dollar weddings. I find this fascinating. Sometimes I'll look at each couple and try to figure out what will go wrong with their marriage. It's not that I want these marriages to fail; we just know they do based on statistics. So it's fun to kind of be a sleuth in the beginning. You can always see when a groom thinks he's big stuff and might have an affair. Or is already having one. Or the bride is all into Herself. I don't get to investigate this too long before a nurse calls me.

"Mary Beth Green."

I'm glad to get this over. The nurse leads me to a room and hands me a paper gown. "Take off your clothes and put this on. Dr. Dorrie will see you shortly."

"All my clothes?"

The nurse nods and gives me this look like she wants to ask what rock I just crawled out from under. Feeling dehumanized, I comply. The room is freezing. I fight the thought that there are hidden cameras in the ceiling vent. Dr. Kelly, what did you get me into? Why do I need a pap smear anyway? People who don't have sex don't need those. I doubt nuns are subjected to them. This is only my second time visiting a gynecologist. I avoid the gynecologist like some people avoid the dentist. But for all I know, there's a giant fungus taking root inside me. Some kind of conspiracy my body summoned against me for never introducing it to a male. I hate the way it sounds, too. *Pap smear.* Smear is such a negative word. For example, *The teacher spent a portion of her day cleaning smeared boogers off desks.* Or, *The girls had a combination of blood and mascara smeared on their faces at the end of the fight.* Smear is never used in a pretty way.

I begin my wait for the doctor.

It's taking a while.

I lean back and close my eyes. The icy air blowing through the vent is probably channeled straight from Antarctica: *Special Delivery to doctors' offices across the globe. From The Coldest Place on Earth!*

When I get cold, I go into hibernation mode. I can't help it. My eyelids are heavy, and I feel myself nodding off. A faraway voice calls my name. I'm like Sleeping Beauty dreaming in the Enchanted Castle, and my prince is standing over me, waiting to kiss me back to life. So I open my eyes, and there he is, just as I imagined he'd always be, with serious brown eyes, concentrating on me. Like I am his only reason to live. This must be what love feels like.

I whisper, "My prince."

"Prince, like the singer?" he says.

Then I realize I'm not dreaming, but awake. And a man is watching me be half-asleep and half-naked.

"Hello, Ms. Green," says the man. "Getting some shut-eye, are we? I apologize for the wait."

It takes me a few seconds to remember I'm in a doctor's office. And the doctor is standing over me. He's got the white jacket and all, stethoscope dangling from his neck. Wiping his eyeglasses on his coat before settling them on his face. Smelling like he just braved a hurricane of coffee and soap.

"I'm Dr. Dorrie," he says, extending his hand for a shake.

I slowly sit up, unfolding like a rusty beach chair, and extend my hand. My heart is still pounding because of my dream, and I feel so exposed. He looks friendly enough. In fact, I feel like I already know him. But I was expecting a woman. At least I asked for a woman doctor.

I sit up a little straighter, pulling the gown around me, careful not to tear the paper, and focus my eyes on him. Then it comes to me that I actually know this man, and not just from my dream. A combination of embarrassment and anger starts forming in my throat and cheeks. I frown at him, searching for words.

"Ms. Green? Are you okay?"

I nod, thinking I should grab my clothes and run.

"Will this be your first mammogram? You seem really nervous," he says, looking at his chart, briefly glancing up. "It won't be so bad. We are very proud to be one of the few OB/GYN offices in North Carolina to offer this service in-house. You indicated that you'd prefer a female physician, so it looks like Dr. Salander will be seeing you. Unfortunately she is running behind today so I thought I'd stick my head in the door and introduce myself, go ahead and get the ball rolling by addressing any concerns you may have. Will you allow that?"

I nod.

"Everything seem relatively normal?"

"Normal?"

"Normal, as in menstrual cycles, or irregularities of that nature."

"Oh." I nod again while he writes on my chart.

"Is there a particular reason why we are seeing you today? Or is this your yearly?"

I don't want to tell Dr. Dorrie about the Dr. Kelly Challenge or that I don't normally have a yearly, but I just say, "Yearly."

"Okay. Great. In that case, Dr. Salander shouldn't be too much longer."

I nod at the man I just called my prince. I could cry. I'm naked, talking

32

to the Jersey Guy about my period. His dog is stashed at my house.

"And if we need to contact you concerning any of the results, when would be best—morning or afternoon?" He writes on a pad of paper. "Afternoon? I'll put a note in your file."

When he finishes making notes, he sets down my file and turns his gaze on me. He doesn't look unkind, or even weary. In fact, he's got a freshly showered, first cup of coffee, inquisitive expression, like the day is new and there's so much to learn.

"You look familiar," he says. "Have we met, Ms. Green?"

Finding my voice I tell him no, we do not know one another at all, but people often tell me I look like Reese Witherspoon.

He blinks. "Who?"

"You know, *Legally Blonde*?"

"That could be it," says Dr. Dorrie, looking at the ceiling like he hasn't watched a movie in eons. "Where do you work? The Green Bean? Gourmet Gourmand? Grocery store, maybe?"

He's trying to place me. "No," I say. "I rarely go to any of those places. Hardly ever."

He crosses his arms and nods.

"I run a boarding house on Main Street, you know, rent out the rooms. I also open up my home during the day as a coffee house of sorts, and hold a meeting on Wednesdays. It's just my thing."

I left out the part about volunteer preschool driver. Just in case he decided to ask, *Oh really? Where's your route? What kind of car do you drive? Have you seen a white poodle with nasty pink stuff around its mouth?*

"On Main Street?" He pronounces each word slowly, giving emphasis to the word *Main*. "I love those old Victorian homes."

"Mine isn't Victorian."

"Not Victorian. Hmm. Let's see, there are a few bungalows, Queen Annes, and Cape Cods. You look like a Cape Cod woman."

I shake my head with a smile.

He continues. "A couple of Prairie Styles, a really neat Italianate, and then there's the house somebody tore down and built a urology clinic in its place. Maybe you live there."

It takes me a second to realize he's joking. "Yes, as a matter of fact I do live in the urology clinic. Great guess."

"Never a dull moment around the dinner table, I suspect."

"It's a ton of fun," I say. "On Chili Night we eat out of bedpans."

He doesn't laugh. He just looks at me over his glasses. I can't believe I said that thing about the bedpans.

"How festive," he says with a smile. "You must sleep on the examination tables there, too."

"That's why I fell asleep in here. I feel right at home," I say gripping the sides of the table.

This time he laughs, and says, "Okay, lady. You gonna tell me where you live? Or do I have to look in your file?"

"You're going to have to look in my file." I can't tell him where I live.

"Seriously?"

He opens my file. Dangit. I didn't think he would.

"303? Is that near the top of the hill?"

I nod.

"Good-looking place. Someday I'd like to buy a home on Main. Great street with all the big trees and shady sidewalks."

"I doubt you'd have to try too hard to find a home there. Something is always for sale."

"Yeah, yeah. Most of those homes are just way too much house for one person. Not to mention all the work you gotta put into those things."

"Thankfully I've got swarms of people helping me out."

"You're fortunate," says Dr. Dorrie. "Out of curiosity…"

"What?" I ask. Please, please don't ask if I've seen a white poodle. Who's now blue.

"You don't by any chance have the original plans to your home do

34

you? I would love to get a look at those. I studied architecture at one time and still love to see the crazy things the old-timers drew into the plans. Hidden rooms and funky spaces."

"Well, I'm not sure," I say, shivering in my gown and trying to suck in my chest as much as possible so Dr. Dorrie doesn't notice how very cold I am.

"You know," he says, "they used to put the house plans in the banister post at the foot of the stairs. It's true. Sometimes you can just lift up the finial, look down inside and pull them out."

I tell him I've never checked, but if I do I'll let him know if I find the plans. I just want out of here.

Dr. Dorrie gives me a nod. "Hey, when did you say that meeting of yours is?"

Crap.

"Wednesday nights. It's boring, though. You probably wouldn't like it." See, I always feel guilty about excluding people from Share Group, so I end up inviting them, anyway. Even the very *last* person I'd want to come. "But you can come if you want."

"Thank you, Ms. Green. I just might do that." He smiles and extends his hand for a shake. "Hang tight. Dr. Salander will be right in."

7

THE TOTALLY PERSONAL DIARY
OF MARY BETH GREEN

June 2, 1990

Dear Diary,

Hello, Brightleaf. Hello, blue room. I'm sitting here on the feather bed I
sleep in every summer and promising myself to keep this diary so that
when I grow up, I will remember what it's like to be 12. Especially if I
have a daughter who is 12. I will not be drunk and crying all the time
with long strings of snot tangled in my pearls, or snooty when I'm sober,
but instead bake lots of carrot cakes and meatloafs. Our house will always
smell like cinnamon and garlic, and I will sit down with a cup of regular
coffee every morning and eat bacon and raisin bran with my daughter.
Yesterday was the last day of the 7th grade, and I left Atlanta at 8:04 p.m.
on the Amtrak. I rode in a sleeper car with a bunk bed and a little toilet
and listened to the mix tape Marcelle made. Marcelle never makes me

tapes, and it is the best tape ever. Somehow Marcelle knows about music that none of my friends have. So I listened to The Pogues, They Might Be Giants, and The Cocteau Twins until ten. Then MC Hammer (who everybody knows). And later I switched to my New Kids On The Block tape. I tried staying awake all night, but the moving of the train always rocks me to sleep like a little baby. My train got to Greensboro at 4:43 in the morning, and Grandmother was waiting for me. It was still nighttime, and she was standing under a light pole wearing one of her outfits from the 1960s again.

It took us a whole forty-five minutes to drive to Brightleaf in her prehistoric Roadmaster. I like it that Marcelle didn't come this time, for the first time ever. I am plenty glad she decided to move into her summer school dorm early. Mainly because whenever a boy talks to me, like at the grocery store or the movies, she ruins it by stepping between me and the boy and saying something stupid just to get attention. But she knows what she's really saying is, Look. Here is a prettier girl, a taller girl… a more sophisticated version of the one you are now talking to. With boobs! I am shocked that middle school boys notice that type thing. But it's true. They do. I don't even like boys, anyway, except two. I wish I could figure out a way to make them notice me. I thought about sending them secret letters so that they would have to guess which girl liked them, and they would look around real hard at all the girls they knew. That would make them look real hard at me. Like, was I the one who sent such a mysterious and exciting letter? But all I'm brave enough to do is call them on the phone and hang up. It is amazing how fast a 7th grade boy can run. I had to race one on field day last year. It was puny little harelip Huey French (he does not speak French). I was so sure I would beat him, but he just took off. Like the Roadrunner. Beep-beep. I never had a chance. He made me feel as slow as Judy Carmichael, who is slower than a sick turtle and has the tiniest teeth in the world. I would never tell another soul, but Huey's speed *shocked me so much, I got a crush on him. Sometimes I would watch him wearing his young Indiana Jones hat to school (which I used to think was pretty dumb) and had the private knowledge that he's a lot stronger than he looks. His scarred lip made him more mysterious. Like a battle wound. If anybody reads this and dares breathe a word, you can guarantee I will put Nair hair removal cream on your eyebrows while you are in a deep sleep. And maybe even on certain spots on your head so it will look like your hair is falling out in clumps, and everyone will think you are dying....X*

8

THE MIND OF MAVIS

My whole name is Billy Mavis Turnkey. Named after my daddy, Billy Mabry. My mama never would agree to marry Billy Mabry, but she sure was crazy about him. She said that just knowin he was willin to get hitched was enough for her, but she didn't never want to marry a man who had regular standing jail time from March to June. Daddy's Spring Fever is what Mama called it. Anyway, Mama always called me Billy May, but all the children in town called me Turkey. Gobble gobble. When I left home at fifteen to run off with Cleavon, I started going by Mavis and kept the Turnkey part.

The Goodwill had a book called *The Poodle Almanac,* and I bought it for three dollars. It tells me near everythang a girl could hope to know about a poodle. What all and what not to feed it. (Never, ever feed a poodle onions or chocolate.) I also learnt poodles is famous at fetchin stuff. I'm teachin Floyd here how to fetch. And I'm pretty much in charge of his groomin, seein that he don't get the mange, and makin sure his roots is touched up. If that evil pervert wasn't lookin for him, I'd let his dye job grow out. Don't get me wrong, blue on a dog is purty, but too much beauty can be a dangerous thang.

I should know. You may think I got it happenin now, but you shoulda seen me in my younger days. I was the belle of the bar. I seen good times and bad, like most ever'one my age. I know what it is to lose a child. When my Orin was born, I looked into his soft lil face and told him he'd be nothin like his daddy, that damn fool Cleavon, who liked to fight and start fires.

When I first took up with Cleavon, it was love at first sight, only I didn't realize he wasn't too bright in the head, and come to find out he had the IQ of a worm, for real. That's what that doctor told me after it was all said and done. By "said and done" what I mean is this: Orin was the spittin image of his daddy in every way, so handsome, but a pyromaniac from birth...and the boy didn't live no longer than eight years. One of the few days his idiot of a daddy was supposed to be watchin him, the shrimp got into the matches and burnt down the trailer with his own self in it. How could I have stopped it? By not being so fool to think he'd be safe with Cleavon. The sadness at losin that boy was almost too much to bear, and I blame nobody but myself. But I have to believe he's in a better place now, livin the life of an angel, far away from Cleavon, who's in Hell.

There's no replacin a lost child, but you can always have other children to love on, which I never did do. Floyd is like a son to me now.

Me and Mary Beth is here at the G.P. We gotta get some of this food home and into the deep freeze before it melts, so we're speed-loadin the conveyor belt at the checkout. Frozen sausage links. Frozen fried chicken. Frozen corn. Frozen lasagna. Beep, beep, beep. Jumbo tea bags. Beep. Super-sized can of coffee. Beep. Hungry Jacks. Beep. Hungry Jacks. Beep. Hungry Jacks. Beep. Hungry Jacks. Beep.

"Well, babe, looks like the last of 'em. Go on now and pick up your magazine. I got it under control," I says.

Mary Beth don't ever want to pay to read her magazine, seein she can cut to the article she's most innerested in pretty fast and be finished by the time the food is bagged. Right now, she done found a story about movie stars who wear the same dress to the same party. For some reason that ain't cool in Hollywood, but if I met someone with the same outfit on as me, Lord, I would love that. While I'm waitin for the cashier to finish ringin us up and baggin our stuff, I cross my arms and hold up my boobs.

"Ah!" says a voice real close. " I can see you are a no-nonsense type, who doesn't follow trends. I can also tell that you are a person open to new ideas and experiences. A refreshing trait, indeed."

I turn around, and there's a man with a teeny mustache and tinier lips. Cute as a caterpillar. His eyes is nice and wide apart, a sign his mama and daddy ain't brother and sister. Even though one of his eyes drifts, I know he's talkin to me cuz his good eye is fixed.

Lord, he just read my mail. I'm shocked a stranger could figure that stuff out about me. So I says, "Do you have ESP or somethin?"

Mary Beth sets down her *People* and looks at him. She says, "Mavis, why should he have ESP?"

"Well, I want to know," I says. "You ain't that psychic who used to come on Oprah?" Law, I hope he is. Cuz I would love to have me a tarot card read or hear about all my different lives. I coulda been a damsel in distress or a grave robber. A princess would be easy, but I hear grave robbin is hard work. Either way I'd get me some good jewelry.

"No, my dear," says that man. "I have never met Oprah, although it would be a grand privilege. I'll have you know that I'm not reading your mind, but I cannot help but have the pleasure of reading your groceries."

"I hope that ain't like palm readin," I says. "Cuz Mary Beth says that's of the devil. Right, MB?" I glance over at Mary Beth.

"That's right. We don't believe in that."

The little wanderin eye lands on Mary Beth while the regular eye looks at me.

"I assure you, I'm no clairvoyant. I have only been gifted with the uncanny knack of understanding certain things about a person based upon their groceries and sundries. Even things they themselves may not be aware of. Not excluding how long a person will live."

"Well, don't be readin mine that way," I says. "I don't want to know when I'm gonna die. I want it to be a surprise."

I look over at Mary Beth, who is lookin at this man, tryin to decide what to make of him. But I've made up my mind. He's gifted is all. How else would he know I don't follow styles?

Mary Beth says, "You're not from Brightleaf are you?"

"Doyle Stubb at your service," he says, holdin out his hand for a shake.

I gotta say he has the most beautiful hands I've ever seen on a man. Such pale, smooth skin, like a baby's, and fangernails so shiny and trimmed, you'd think he spends his days sortin through feathers and cotton balls. And believe me when I say I've seen fangernails on a man that would scare the shit out of Dracula.

Doyle says, "I recently moved to Brightleaf from Phoenix, Arizona. My mother is quite ill in The Peaceful Future Nursing Home."

"I'm sorry to hear about your mama," I says. "Phoenix, Arizona? Ain't that all hot and cactusy?"

"My dear," says Doyle, "Arizona has a most pleasant climate. Though it can be hot, it is quite arid, which is marvelous."

Right away, I know this is a good man. He came clear across the country to be with his mama. So I says to Doyle, "Doyle, you got a place to stay? Cuz Mary Beth here owns a boardin house, and we could use an extra man about." I look at Mary Beth and nod to her like we have twin minds and she'd agree to it, but her lips get real tight, and she's givin me the look that says she don't want me goin around offering no psychics a place to stay.

Mary Beth says, "Well, Mr. Stubbs…"

"Stubb…it's Stubb. And please, call me Doyle."

42

"Okay, Doyle," says Mary Beth. "Seeing I've only just met you, I can't say I feel comfortable renting to you just yet. But I would love for you to come by the house for a cup of coffee or join us on Wednesday night for Share Group."

"I thank you kind ladies very much for showing concern for my well-being," says Doyle. "But I already have a nice cottage not far from here. The invitation for coffee and whatnot is equally appealing. You shall see me soon," says Doyle as he runs his finger over his mustache, and looks real hard at those bagged groceries in our cart.

Mary Beth

I felt like throwing a blanket over our groceries. I did not want him looking at them that way. It seemed almost like he could see through our clothes. Figure out all the combinations on our locks, our social security numbers, and even the secrets we keep from our own selves. Anyway how hard can it be to estimate how long someone will live by looking in his shopping cart? If someone has a buggy packed with beer and Twinkies it's no mystery they probably won't make it to one hundred. You don't have to be magic to know that.

9

MANCHILD

Mavis

Manchild shows up at the house every day but Wednesdays—to dodge the sharin time. I told him I don't want him comin around ever. He's crazy about me, but ever since Cleavon's been long dead I don't wanna be worryin about no man. Sure, I have men friends that I shoot the breeze with here and there, have a smoke with and all. I don't mind me some attention. So when I seen Manchild giving me the sly wink, I says, "Hey baby, ain't you cute?" I wasn't thinkin of being his girlfriend or nothin, just friendly flirtin is all. He's twenty-seven, so I'm old enough to be his gramaw.

That Manchild is hard to shake, though. Followin me from in front when I walk down the street to the Goodwill. Walkin backward, makin a fool of hisself, laughin like he's so funny, but his eyes is sad. Some people always look sad, even when they ain't. For some reason, he reminds me of my own little Orin. But his missin teeth tell me he don't like to brush. Orin brushed.

I'm missin teeth myself, on the bottom. I'll be the first to say, but mine are gone cuz my mama got me dippin at a early age, to get me to calm down when I was fussy. I took up smokin at the age of twelve cuz it's a lot easier to look glamorous for the boys smokin a cigarette instead of dippin snuff and lookin like you been chewin on cat turds all day.

I might not be college educated like Mary Beth, but I've been around the block a few times, and I can tell that Manchild is bad news. I ain't sure what all kinds of drugs he's on, but he is on disability. I already had me a taste of that disability sugar with Cleavon. He was always gettin jobs on the sly and hidin it from the government, so he could keep two checks. Anyway, Mary Beth says her grandma told her that a man is like a Bible prophecy: Sweet in the mouth, but bitter in the belly. I ain't sure exactly what that means, but I suspect it's somethin like: Fun to kiss, but don't get knocked up. That's some good advice.

10

THE TRAFFIC LIGHT

Mary Beth

I've got four kids packed into the Subaru, one in the front and three in the back, and we're bound for Toddlers Are People, Too. The biggest pain about driving the carpool is strapping those toddler boosters in every single school day, but like I said, I just want to lend a hand. Dr. Kelly is on the radio, and I'm fixing to see what kind of advice she's gonna give to the woman who just called in. The Doctor Kelly Show is like Jerry Springer, only you don't have the advantage of actually seeing what the guests look like. On television, when the guests come traipsing out on stage, the audience immediately knows they've got a special case on their hands. The anxiety starts building the moment you lay eyes on the puny, goateed boyfriend. It seems like the boyfriend isn't fully formed yet, like he's stuck in some kind of metamorphosis between tadpole and man. Then the wife or girlfriend stomps out looking like a sumo wrestler, wearing a bikini top and low-slung shorts, with a bunch of Chinese letters tattooed across her chest. A lot of people get real emotional about Asian lettering, as if anything written in Chinese must embody all that is peaceful, or yin yang, or feng shui, but for all they know, that tattoo says something real terrible in Chinese, like "puppy eater." I'm just saying, if I need an interpreter to read it, it's not gonna get permanently stamped into my skin.

Dr. Kelly's latest caller says, "Dr. Kelly, my husband is paralyzed from the waist down. I feel like he should help with the dishes since his arms work…"

I can't stand it anymore. I click off the AM station and push in my Linda Ronstadt's Greatest Hits tape. I fast forward to my favorite song and start singing, "You and I travel to the beat of a different drum, Oh, can't you tell by the way I run, every time you make eyes at me." I belt it out to the toddlers, while they clap their chubby hands. "And I ain't sayin' you ain't pretty, All I'm saying is I'm not ready—" When I'm distracted by something in my rearview mirror. Linda and I are going to have to pick this up later because I'm being tailgated again. By the same individual as always. At the red light, I stop and he stops behind me. I put the car in park, roll down the windows, and remove the key. In the words of the monkey from the Lion King, It is time.

I turn to the toddlers and say, "Just a minute. Miss Mary Beth is gonna take care of a little business." Then I shut the door and walk to the driver's side door of the car behind me, and rap firmly on his window. He looks at me over his glasses and rolls down the window.

"Hello, Dr. Dorrie," I say. "Fancy seeing you here at the light, so close behind me."

"Do I know you?" he asks.

I keep my composure, even though he does indeed know me. He's seen me in nothing but a paper gown. I realize he's got several mental hurdles that must affect him every minute of every day, so I help him by removing my sunglasses and say, "I'm one of your patients, Mary Beth Green."

"Cape Cod?"

"Nooo."

The light turns green and the cars behind us start honking, and driving around us. About that same time Dr. Dorrie's face breaks out into this huge smile and he says, "Juuust kidding. How could I forget you? Getting enough sleep these days?"

"What?"

"You were catching some winks when I walked into the exam room. Remember?"

I shake my head and I say, "I wouldn't have fallen asleep if you didn't make me wait so long in a freezing exam room. In a paper gown. Ya'll should get some real robes. Or fur coats. It's way too cold in there. Anyway, I could have fallen off that examination table and cracked my head wide open." Then I take a deep breath and continue. "Also could you please not follow me so closely? It makes me nervous." There, I said it. It feels so great to tell Dr. Jersey that he is the one who is making me wait, that he is the one who is causing me distress. It's not the other way around, like he always acts. My face is hot and my heart is pounding.

Dr. Dorrie takes off his glasses, wipes them, and puts them back on, like he's thinking. Then he says, "I didn't realize you felt unsafe during your appointment. I'll talk to Dr. Salander about putting some pads on the floor, or maybe employing the belt to strap you in. We don't normally use that, because patients are more comfortable without it, but I never thought much about the possibility of women falling off the table and injuring themselves. The patient's comfort and safety is a high priority for us. Cotton robes are also a good suggestion."

I nod and feel myself softening. Good God. Where is my resolve?

I hear myself saying, "I probably wouldn't have fallen off, since I've got very good slumbering balance, but others may not be so lucky."

Dr. Dorrie smiles and says, "Not everyone has good slumbering balance."

I can't help but notice how smooth his face is and what a pleasant smile he has. I need to get a hold of myself. I remind myself of all those New Jersey line-breakers, and shake my head in disgust.

Then he says, "Hey, it's been great talking with you. I've gotta get back to the office, but thanks for the good advice. Also, you should get your lights fixed. It's very dangerous like that. I can't tell when you're gonna slow down, so I end up having to slam on brakes every few seconds."

"My lights?"

"Yeah, both your brake lights are out. I just realized I've been behind your car on countless mornings on my way to the office. Sometimes I leave a little later to avoid you. Weird."

"It is weird," I nod, twisting my keys. "Small world."

"So it's a good thing you stopped," he says. "And I'm glad to know it's you driving the car instead of some neurotic road-rager who might shoot me or slash my tires."

I laugh a little too hard and say, "Me too. I'm glad it's just me." Then I remember it's not just me. "The toddlers!" I run and jump in my car, put it in gear and crawl to the preschool, taking back streets. I look in my rearview mirror. Dr. Dorrie is following me. When I pull into the parking lot of Toddlers Are People, Too, he salutes me. As he drives away, I wonder if he was serious when he mentioned strapping me to the table.

11

BRIGHTLEAF R.F.D

June 14, 1990

Dear Diary,

Like on the Andy Griffith reruns, R.F.D. stands for Rural Free Delivery. In other words, B.L.T.-- Boring Little Town. Grandmother took me shopping at Dundy's for a few things, but what I wouldn't give for a new baby doll dress and a pair of acid washed jeans. I won't be caught dead in the Little Mermaid swimsuit she picked out for me. She told me all the other swimsuits were too immodest for a girl my age. Forget the Brightleaf pool this summer. Grandmother has no cable, so there's nothing to do but watch PBS and Lawrence Welk reruns on the local channel. That's why I'm up here, writing again. Sometime I guess I'll confess the Huey Incident. I would probably still be secretly in awe of Huey if he didn't get too big for his britches and muscle ahead of me in the cafeteria and take the last chocolate pudding. Huey probably saw me standing there and said to himself, *There's that slow girl I beat on field day, so I'm going to get in front of her.* That decided it. I did not secretly want to know how strong Huey was anymore. The harelip lost its charm. Grandmother is knocking and wants me to go to a flea market with her and her old lady friends. The flea market beats watching the white guy with the afro paint pictures on public television. The Huey Incident will be continued....X

12

SHARE GROUP #2

Mary Beth

It's Wednesday night again. We finished eating and are pulling chairs around for Share Group. Those who didn't come for dinner are just arriving. Angus is here. His eyes are more bloodshot than usual. Jimmy, Winslow, Mavis, Eleanor, Vanessa and Ned are sitting in the circle. Vanessa is smiling and showing off the new gold star on her front tooth. She comes here once a week and cleans the whole downstairs, mops, dusts, and kills spiders. She won't accept a dime for her work. I'd be more than happy to pay her because this is a woman who knows how to clean. Finding good household help is like stumbling upon a diamond in a pile of zirconia. Vanessa could definitely be one of those angels.

We sit down and prepare to free our minds to share when the doorbell rings. No one rings the doorbell here; everyone just lets themselves in. I start worrying it might be the police catching up with me about a dognapping. Eleanor hops up to answer it, and I pour myself another cup of coffee.

We hear Eleanor and another voice echoing in the foyer, then footsteps in our direction. I hear a man's voice saying, "I heard you give regular tours."

"I'm not sure, but I can ask Mary Beth," says Eleanor.

Eleanor walks into the room followed by Dr. Dorrie. I about drop my coffee cup on the floor. He looks clean and fit in blue jeans and a t-shirt. He walks towards me with his hand out-stretched for a shake and says, "Mary Beth? Right?" Then he realizes there is a circle of people staring at him.

"Whoops," he says. "Looks like you guys are having a meeting. I didn't realize it was this organized when you invited me."

I cannot believe my eyes. The Jersey Guy is here. In my very home. Floyd's home. I invited him.

Boy, am I in trouble.

Flustered, I say as cheerfully as I can, "Why yes, Doctor! So glad you came!" I shake his hand.

"You mentioned something about an open house on Wednesdays, so I thought I'd check it out," says Dr. Dorrie.

I totally doubted he would come.

I look around the room, hoping to God that Floyd stays put, wherever he is. I say, "Everyone, this is the Jers—Dr. Terry Dorrie. I met him the other day and invited him to come over and see the house."

"Hey Doc, have a seat," says Jimmy pulling up a chair.

"Thanks," says Dr. Dorrie.

"Dr. Dorrie, we were just getting ready to have our Share Group session," I say. "This is normally what we do on Wednesday nights. I guess I didn't make that clear."

"It's Terry," he says. He sits down halfway, like he may not stay and says, "Is this group therapy or something? I can come back another time if you want."

Here is my chance to send him on his way, to save my butt, to make sure Floyd is nowhere around next time he comes.

"No, no," I say. "This is not professional group therapy. You're welcome to stay, and afterwards I'll show you around."

"Great." He sits back down and gestures for me to carry on.

I take a brief moment to explain the rules of Share Group again, and we begin in silence. I have trouble relaxing. I want to shoot out of my chair, find Floyd and stick him in the backyard with a muzzle. I decide he's probably sleeping in Mavis's room, so I look at my scripture verses on the wall and wait for someone to say something.

"So what kind of doctor are you?" asks Winslow. "Academic or medicine?"

"Medical," says Dr. Dorrie.

If he'd said gynecologist, everyone would automatically conclude he'd seen me naked.

"What kind of medicine?" asks Winslow.

"OB/GYN."

All eyes turn on me.

Vanessa says, "Mary Beth, you pregnant?"

"I am not pregnant. I assure you I am not."

"Did you think you was pregnant? I never even knew you had you a boyfriend." She scans the circle, trying to figure out if I could be dating one of the men present: Angus, Jimmy, Winslow or Ned. Certainly not the Jersey Guy. Everyone else starts looking around too. Wondering.

I say, "Remember when I shared how I was going to get a mammogram? The one Dr. Kelly begged everyone to get?"

Automatically everyone stares at my breasts. Now I'm positive everyone thinks Dr. Dorrie has seen me naked. The men are all kind of smiling. And so is Dr. Dorrie. Then I say, "Well, ladies, ya'll need to go get one, too. And hurry up."

"I hope it ain't too late to get that shirt, This Mamma Got Her Mammo," says Mavis.

"If it's too late, you can have mine," I say.

Things get quiet again.

"I've had irregular pap smears for the last ten years," Eleanor says, staring at the floor.

Winslow says, "I could help you get them more regularly. I'm a doctor."

"Psychologists don't give pap smears, you warped thing," says Vanessa.

Mavis pipes up, "Well, you'd probably be more regular if you ate somethin more nutritional than coffee and lettuce."

"Your irregularity could be caused by a number of things," says Dr. Dorrie. "Who's your gynecologist?"

"Patterson."

"Is Dr. Patterson concerned about this?"

"It's hard to tell," says Eleanor.

"Tell you what, let's talk about this later. Maybe I could call Dr. Patterson and we could discuss it, if it would help you feel better. I believe we can get to the bottom of this."

"No pun intended," mumbles Winslow.

I feel bad for Terry Dorrie. I bet he's wondering what kind of Confederate freak show he's wandered into. I've got to think of a way to change course. But before I say anything, he sneezes twice.

"Bless you, Dr. Dorrie."

"Thankyaaa-choo! Achoo!"

"Catchin cold?" asks Mavis.

"I don't think so. I felt perfectly fine when I walked in. You must have a pet of some sort here. I'm highly allergic to animal dander."

Mavis opens her mouth and says, "As a matter of fact, we've got ourselves a poor little poodle we saved from an abusive pervert. Only, the Poodle Almanac says poodles is one of the least allergic dogs in the world."

"'Cause poodles don't shed!" says Jimmy.

"The Poodle Almanac says that poodles do shed," says Mavis. "Their hairs just don't fall all over the floor like a lot of animals' fur does. It stays on them. The old fur sticks to the dog. But that don't mean it won't make somebody start sneezin."

"An abusive pervert?" says Terry Dorrie.

Mavis says, "Mary Beth is a hero. She brought him home, and he was white–"

"White with fear," I cut in and give Mavis a look. "Yes," I continue. "Poor Floyd was white with fear when we found him."

"How can a dog be white with fear?" asks Dr. Dorrie.

"Well, Terry, you've got to be a dog lover to detect a certain pallor about them at times. The whites of their eyes are…whiter, more gel-like."

"Gel-like, ay?"

"Yes."

"Okay, I just learned something new. You know I had a poodle myself, and he was white, except not with fear. Just white. He got out of his fence and I haven't seen him in a few weeks."

Now, as if on cue, Floyd begins to whimper at the kitchen door. Great.

"That must be the fearful one now," says Dr. Dorrie, laughing. "It's okay, you can let him out."

"I don't think that would be a good idea," I say. "Floyd is petrified of strangers and he might pee on the floor."

"Nonsense," says Mavis. "Floyd ain't never met a stranger."

With this, she opens the swinging kitchen door. Floyd stands there with his new Midnight Blue hairdo and looks at Dr. Dorrie.

"I may be allergic," says Dr. Dorrie, "but I've definitely got a way with dogs. So it's Floyd, huh? Come 'ere Floyd," he calls, patting his knee.

I give Floyd a look that says *if you go to him I'll tie bows in your hair*.

Floyd ignores me and streaks out of the kitchen in a blur of blueness right onto Dr. Dorrie's lap.

"Hey boy…wow, you're fast. Almost as fast as my dog. Maybe faster."

Dr. Dorrie scratches behind Floyd's ears, and his eyes land on the rose tattoo.

"What? Is this dog a member of the Russian Mafia?"

Floyd whimpers and licks Dr. Dorrie's hand and face and sits in his lap until Dr. Dorrie breaks out into a full blown sneezing attack and has to place him on the floor.

Around nine, we call it a night. Before Dr. Dorrie goes home, he bangs on the banister a little to see if it's hollow and then pokes his head in the kitchen to say good-bye to Floyd, promising to bring him a doggie treat on his next visit.

Next visit? Why would he come back?

Tonight was a close call.

A strange night, too.

13

DOYLE STUBB

Mavis

Manchild, he done gave up on me cuz I quit talkin to him. He's got hisself a new love now. Eleanor done made the mistake of feelin sorry for him and bought him a iPad to get him real professional, so he could get a regular job. First he watched a whole bunch of porno on the iPad, then he hocked it at the pawn shop. It sure did make him feel loved to get a present.

I'm fixin the food for the Share time when I hear Dr. Dorrie talkin out in the Great Room. "Hey there, Yankee!" I yell out the kitchen door. "Come on in and make yourself at home."

I told Dr. D he can call me Trailer Trash, since I like to call him Yankee. But he gets this real bothered look on his face and won't do it. Last time he said, "Mavis, I could never call you that. *Trash* should never be applied to *anyone*." (He takes it real serious.) "If I had to call you Trailer anything it'd be Trailer *Treasure*."

That's real sweet and all, but he's got to learn to take a joke. Loosen up, baby. And if you're gonna give me a nickname with *Trailer* in it, I'm very partial to *Twilight Trailer* cuz I did read them Vampire books. And they was goooood.

Dr. D swings open the kitchen door. He's been comin to the Share Group for a few weeks now and taken to comin early to help me fix supper and set up the furniture. He's got on a t-shirt and jeans. He likes to pull up a chair at the kitchen table and talk while I'm cookin. He's told me a little about hisself.

First off, Dr. D was going to be an architect. He went to some fancy design college in Chicago. But when his mama, who he was devoted to, got real sick and died of some kind of lady cancer, he decided to go into medicine. Doc's a natural born gynecologist. That lady doctor who works with him is for prisspots, like Mary Beth. But for folks like me who would much rather have a man gynecologist, he is happy to oblige. Don't be gettin no strange notions – Dr. D is professional.

Some thangs I learned about Dr. D: He grew up in New Jersey. They don't drink sweet tea up yonder. Dr. D is divorced. He was once married to a lady who ran out on him. She wrote him a note sayin how she needed some adventure and left him her dog.

Doc thinks he's helpin with supper by bringin over kitchen tools. So now I got me a new garlic press, meat thermometer, apple corer, egg timer and a julienne maker (whatever). Stuff like that. I always says *thank you*, but I don't have the heart to tell him I won't never use any of that junk. What I want to say to Dr. D is, *Get your sweet buns down to the Sam's Club, and pick me up a jumbo bag of instant mashed potatoes, a fifty-pack of frozen burgers, and a ten-pound bag of shredded cheddar.* Now that would make sense.

Sometimes when we're sittin around the table talkin, Eleanor sticks her skinny head in the door and looks. If Doc's in the middle of sayin somethin, he shuts right up sayin what he was sayin and turns to Eleanor in a doctor-like way and says, "Well, hello Eleanor. How have you been feeling lately?"

Eleanor says she's doing okay and tries to hang out and be a part of what we were doin. She fixes a cup of coffee and tries to look casual and all. She sits down at the table like she's sayin, *I'm cool to hang out with*. But Dr. D usually turns toward her like she's a patient, and he's waitin to hear her tell what all she's ailin from so he can write her a prescription. Doc means well, but Eleanor don't like to be taken like a science project.

The thing I find strangest, Mary Beth don't never come into the kitchen and chat with me and Doc. And he has plenty of questions about her.

"You need to ask Mary Beth them questions."

Winslow coughs and pants his way into the house. I can hear him clear from the kitchen. I walk into the livin room and behold him in his tan joggin outfit, sweat rollin down the sides of his face, chokin like he's fixin to pop a hairball. He holds up a hand and motions for me to hold on till he catches his breath. Then he reaches in his pocket with the other hand and pulls him out a cigarette.

I cross my arms and wait for his coughin to die out. Then he lights up. Mary Beth don't like people smokin in the house, but I ain't the smoke police.

"You better quit that before you have a heart attack."

He takes a drag and shakes his head.

"I ain't talkin about smokin. Quit that joggin."

"I need to do it," he says after blowin out smoke. "Keeps my heart and lungs strong."

"Hmpf. Smokin and exercise don't mix."

"Actually, Mavis, you ought to seriously think about going out for a jog yourself."

"I suspect you're thinkin more about how my girls here would look bobbin up and down in a tank top than my general health."

"It would be a pleasure to have a jogging buddy," says Winslow. "Especially an attractive older woman like yourself."

"Older woman, my ass," I says "I ain't got but fifteen years on you."

Winslow laughs and jerks into another fit of coughin.

Most everyone is startin to trickle in the house for the sharin time. The ones that didn't come for supper is settlin themselves down, includin Doyle.

Doyle! It's his first time, and he just sorta slipped in without anybody seein him. But here he is, lookin like he's gettin ready to do somethin otherworldly. I've only met the man one single time in my life, but I feel like he's one of the most unusual people I've ever met. If he had him a fan club, like Michael Bublé, I'd be his biggest fan.

I says, "Why Doyle Stubb, you sly thang. How'd you get past the security?" I point at Floyd, who's prancin around the inside of the circle gettin friendly with everyone. It's a joke about Floyd being security.

Doyle smiles with his tiny lips and looks at me real cheerful outta the good eye and says, "Perhaps the dog is more selective than you think."

I swear, that man is cool as all get-out.

"Doyle, what do you mean by *selective*?"

"Have you ever seen the dog shy away from anyone?" he asks.

"Come to think of it, Floyd won't go near Manchild. What are you gettin at? Floyd reads people like you read them groceries?"

"Dogs are quite different. Their animal instincts work constantly, which humans, although we possess them, don't normally allow to operate."

"So you think Floyd's got *ESP*?"

Everybody, except Mary Beth, who's in the kitchen, quits talkin and listens to Doyle.

"When I approach a home," says Doyle, slowly movin his hands like he's touchin an invisible wall, "I prepare myself for the possible presence of an animal by letting my defenses down and opening my senses up to them."

Now he's usin his hands to stir the air, and he's sniffin like he's a hound dog, his mustache twitchin.

"Your Floyd accepted my spirit and was immediately aware I was no threat to his home."

"You can do that stuff, Floyd?" I says, lookin at Floyd like he's a real genius.

Floyd chews his bottom.

Winslow says, "Yeah, I do that, too." He starts coughin like he's got another hairball, but really he's just tickled with Doyle talkin all serious that way about Floyd.

Mary Beth looks real surprised when she walks outta the kitchen and sees Doyle Stubb bein the center of attention. "Well hello, Mr. Stubb," she says. "Fancy seeing you here. It's been a couple of weeks. I hope your mother is well."

Doyle says, "Thank you for inquiring after mother. She's fighting as valiantly as anyone who cannot remember her own name. I sing Barry Manilow to keep her spirits up, and at times she joins in. To hear her sing 'Copacabana' would bring tears to your eyes."

"I'm so sorry to hear that," says Mary Beth.

"Your concern is touching."

"Well, how in the world did you find the house, considering I don't quite remember giving you directions?"

Doyle says, "My dear, I had no problem finding you, as I could not help but notice the large can of wasp spray in your cart at our last meeting."

Mary Beth looks worried.

Doyle keeps on talkin, "Also, the presence of five packages of toilet tissue and several large frozen lasagnas provided me with a route."

"Do tell," says Mary Beth. She crosses her arms.

Doyle's lazy eye looks at the ceiling, and his regular eye looks at me. He says, "I looked for a house with a large porch, simply because wasps enjoy making nests in them, and a home that is big enough to warrant five bathrooms, as well as a large crowd of people to whom the lasagnas would be served. Several homes fit the description, but then I saw the poodle on the porch, which corresponded to the bag of pet food for 'small and toy-sized dogs.' It was slightly more than a lucky guess."

Mary Beth has a pretty strange look on her face, but she says, "Everyone, this is Mr. Stubb—"

"Call me Doyle. It is a pleasure to meet you all."

"Doyle is new to Brightleaf, but it looks like ya'll have already met him."

"Hey, Doyle."

"What's goin' on, Doyle?"

Doyle shakes hands with Jimmy, Winslow, Vanessa, Ned and Terry.

"Doyle is a particularly talented man," I says. Mary Beth rolls her eyes at me, but I think these folks have the right to know a sensation is in their midst.

"Oh yeah?" says Dr. D. "What are your talents, Doyle?"

Doyle is just standin there chewin on a carrot stick, his tiny lips movin like a rabbit. He don't look like a master at nothin.

I says, "I ain't never seen a man who can mind read like you see in them alien movies, but Doyle is the closest thing to it, next to a real life alien."

"Why thank you, kind lady, that was quite poetic," says Doyle.

Mary Beth

I've never seen, nor heard, Mavis so touched by a person in all my life. I sincerely hope Doyle is not a cult man because if he happened to form his own religion, Mavis would be his first follower. Then I'd lose my cook, but not before Doyle wielded his power to get his eyeballs in my pantry and discover all my secrets. The thought that he could steal my identity just by peeking at my canned goods...

"Well I sure do wish you'd show everyone some of the thangs you can do," says Mavis. "But I guess you'd have to follow every one of us around the supermarket, like you did with me and Mary Beth."

"I was fortunate enough to glimpse your purchases at the checkout," says Doyle, smiling, "but I'm quite astute at reading grocery lists, as well as receipts."

"You need to get you a job with the police," says Mavis. "Crime solvin. Lord, I'd love to know the kinds of foods a killer would buy."

"What can he do, exactly?" asks Winslow.

"Doyle can tell your fortune just by lookin at all the stuff you buy. Right Doyle?" Mavis says.

"Particularly food stuffs, but not limited to," says Doyle, nodding.

Mavis whispers in my ear that it would be very dramatic if we let Doyle do his thing. I'm not sure about any of this hanky-panky, but Mavis reminds me of my scripture on the wall about strangers maybe being angels. So I give a reluctant nod.

Now she goes and whispers in Doyle's ear. Doyle's lazy eye looks like it's assenting and gearing up for action.

Mavis takes charge and says, "I want all ya'll to fish around in your pockets and pocketbooks and find you a grocery list or a receipt, if you got one. Put your name on it, and pass it to Doyle here."

"I'm doubtful," says Vanessa.

"Just you wait," says Mavis.

Jimmy says, "I've got a receipt from last month. It's kind of crumpled, though."

Vanessa says, "Why you got a receipt in your pants pocket from last month? Don't you wash your britches?"

"Why wash them? Paint won't wash out."

Eleanor says she lost all her shopping lists.

Everyone else passes lists or receipts around to Doyle. He pulls Vanessa's out first and studies it.

"Ah, here's a woman, fastidious and tireless, with a heart as golden as her tooth. You will begin a new business venture in the near future. And I see you writing your memoir, which is to be well received. House cleaning will be a thing of the past. I assume that is your current occupation, my dear? You will live long and enjoy your grandchildren, who will bring you nothing but pride."

Even though Vanessa is a black lady, you can tell she's blushing. She asks, "How do you know I clean houses? There ain't no cleaning supplies on that receipt."

"Ahhh," says Doyle, holding up a finger. "No cleaning supplies, but a pair of rubber gloves, a Martha Stewart *Living* Magazine, and a *Soap Opera Digest*. The digest tells me the most about your schedule. That you keep up with the soaps, but can't always. *Living* is known to be a most un-relaxing publication, as it is full of tips on how to keep your home and domestic duties seamless, orderly, and immaculate. Individuals as tireless as yourself flock to it. Oh, my dear. This receipt is rich. The bag of dried kidney beans, the pound of turkey bacon, the jar of pickled beets."

Vanessa has the most curious expression. She holds out her hand for her receipt and puts on her reading glasses for a closer look. She shakes her head and smiles.

Next is Ned. Doyle takes longer to analyze Ned's receipt. He stands there eyeballing each item, then looks up at the ceiling, then at Ned. Finally he frowns and says, "This is dark. Perhaps I should deliver your reading in private? Conversely, you may prefer the presence and comfort of friends. Which do you desire?"

Ned makes this goofy, thinking face, pretending to be scared and all. Then he relaxes and says, "Naw man, hit me. I can handle it."

Both of Doyle's eyes focus steadily on Ned. Then, holding his G.P. receipt with two fingers, Doyle says, "A love for video games and syndicated television will quickly bring doom. However, I see there's a strong chance of success if you can break the addictions. And I mean, IF."

"Cool!" says Ned, more excited than anyone should be. "How'd you know that, dude? Like, what food do I buy that tells you that stuff? Like 'doom'? How *sick* is that!"

Then Ned hugs Doyle. You can tell by Doyle's response, he isn't normally hugged at times like this.

After Ned's hug, Doyle regains his composure and says, "If you are truly curious, it is your purchase of multiple packages of Hot Pockets, combined with boxes of frozen yam patties. Hot Pockets, as a regular meal, are an indicator of a serious gaming addiction, while frozen yam patties are an unnatural product made to *appear* natural, thus the parallel with television—it will never be reality, no matter how strong a bond you feel with a particular character."

"Hot Pockets and yams? Hmmm. But what about the success?" asks Ned.

"Frozen spinach. No one but successful persons eat spinach. Albeit frozen, it's spinach, nonetheless."

"Spinach it will be, then!" says Ned, throwing his arms wide.

Doyle pulls out the next list, and it's mine.

"Hmm. I've seen these groceries before."

I say, "Yes, you saw similar groceries in The Grocery Palace when you met us. Our list rarely varies, Mr. Stubb. And you already used them to tell Mavis her fortune, remember?"

"I do remember. Ah, yes indeed. I could tell that day something was awry as I studied that particular grocery cart. Now I understand. I had *joint* groceries before my eyes."

"*Joint* groceries? What's that supposed to mean?"

"It *means* that I experienced *interference* from your part of the list. A cross-frequency that puzzled me then but is clear now. And I'm seeing *you*. I see that you are a deeply religious woman but hypocritical at times."

"Oh, really?"

"Hmmm," Doyle continues. "Generally accepting of most individuals, yet your heart is divided."

"Divided? I assure you I have a single heart and mind, Mr. Stubb."

Doyle smiles with his teensy lips.

"On the contrary, my dear, your heart is divided between desiring love…and rejecting it."

Somebody gives a low whistle. This is so embarrassing. I neither desire nor reject…what? Love? Give me a break.

I cross my arms, and say to Doyle ever so sweetly, "My goodness, Mr. Stubb. I can't even begin to think what on that grocery list would cause you to formulate such a crazy conclusion."

Doyle keeps on smiling in this sly way and says, "Half and half."

"Half and half?" I say. "Come on, Mr. Stubb, everybody buys half and half. Many of them are happily married people. Or dating, or something."

"Good lady, I would never fabricate such a thing. My gifting is partly scientific, one of the criteria being The Combination. I view the half and half in concurrence with the other products you chose. We all choose certain products for particular, or even *peculiar* reasons, Ms. Green. So to answer your question, my dear, your list is individual *only to you*."

Whatever. This *uninvited* person is inventing stuff about me in front of the whole Share Group. I will stay calm. "Okay, I hear you. Thanks for your interpretation of my groceries, whether we agree on them or not. Anybody dare to go next?"

"It happens to be the doctor's turn," says Doyle, "if he is interested."

Dr. Terry Dorrie looks game. "What will it hurt? Fire away."

"All right, good doctor," says Doyle, holding his receipt.

Doyle eyeballs the receipt and looks at Terry thoughtfully. Looking back at the receipt, Doyle begins to grin. He smiles as wide as he can (which isn't very wide because his mouth is baby doll size).

"Very interesting, indeed. So interesting I'm not sure if I should say."

"Say! Say! Say!" yells Jimmy.

Terry looks genuinely worried. He says, "Either you see or you don't."

"Oh, I assure you, I *see*," nods Doyle.

"Give me back my receipt," says Terry. And he snatches it from Doyle's fingers.

Yay, Terry! Way to fight back. Except that…he really did snatch it. He did not ask for it, hold out his hand or any of that. It was more like the action of a child who wants to protect himself from…what?

Mavis says, "Doyle, why you smilin and not tellin? That might-could make a person feel bad."

It looks to me like Terry isn't up for Doyle to tell, anyway.

"Hey, no fair," says Jimmy. "We want to know. C'mon, Doc, what could be so funny or so *bad* about you? Maybe he was gonna tell us what you and Mavis are cooking back in the kitchen all the time. Or maybe you're a serial killer!"

Everybody laughs.

"Let's go, Doyle," says Winslow. "Hurry up so you can get to Jimmy and me."

Winslow wants his groceries read real bad.

Terry stands up. "I need to get going. I've got an early day tomorrow."

This grocery reading business was a bad idea. As I originally thought. I hate it that a Share Group meeting upset someone. That's the very opposite of what we hope to achieve at our meetings.

Mavis and I follow Terry to the door.

"Are you okay?" I ask. "This didn't really turn out as I planned. I mean…I had no control. I am so sorry you were offended."

Terry opens his mouth to say something but stops.

Mavis says, "C'mon Doc. Nobody's thinkin nothin *bad* about you. Everybody knows we ain't lovers. But I wouldn't mind it a bit."

"It's okay, Mavis," says Terry. "I need to be hitting the road. But thanks for the kind words." And he walks out the door.

"Well, Doyle," says Mavis, "I guess that one came back to bite us in the butt."

14

NOT SO TOP SECRET ENTRY

June 20, 1990

Dear Diary,

There are kids around my age who live in a few houses on Main Street, but I haven't felt like making friends with them yet. They pass me on their bikes like they are in some kind of gang that's required to wear Izod. And I've seen a group of girls about my age smoking cigarettes in the City Park. It's not like I've never smoked a whole pack of Virginia Slims all by myself. So 6th grade. Recently, I've become a real regular in the garage sale circuit. I used to think you'd always find nasty stuff, like somebody's old false teeth or a half-used tube of Chapstick at garage sales. I was right. If you want that kind of stuff it's there for the taking. Some people think it's OK to sell anything. Once I saw some old person's potty-chair with some real pee turned to brown syrup in the bowl. Right in the front yard. Like *the people selling it were darn proud and really lucky to have this quality potty in their sale. Besides the gross stuff, there is a whole bunch of great stuff, too. Yesterday I bought a pair of hot pink Converse high-tops. They fit just right. I also found a really good pocketbook that I paid 2 dollars for, and it still had a bunch of change inside it. $3.47. The old records are the funniest. I bought one for 50 cents, just to see what was on it. Crazy Horses by Donnie and Marie Osmond. My mother wouldn't be caught dead at a flea market. Not even tanked-up. And she would just die if she knew I was walking all over Brightleaf in the shoes of a stranger. It does not bother me at all, as long as I wear socks. The thing that bothers me more than contracting athlete's foot from the last owner of these shoes, is watching Grandmother and her friends dance at their favorite restaurant every week. Smitty's has polka on Friday nights. The band is a group of men with thick glasses and comb-overs playing horns and an accordion. There's a dance floor if you want to dance. And I never do. I'm just there for the meatloaf because I can't seem to get enough of it. As much as I like meatloaf, I would be completely mortified if any of my friends from Atlanta ever saw me walking into Smitty's because everybody knows it's a place old people go to flirt and carry on with each other, which is very disturbing to me....X*

15

A LITTLE PROBLEM

Mary Beth

Somebody knocks on my bedroom door very early in the morning. The rising sun slowly seeps through the blinds, and I'd like to rest here between the sheets feeling the coolness on my legs and think about the coming day before answering that knock. It's Mavis. She's whispering to me through the door. She says we have no running water. I mumble for her to call the city and see if there's a broken line.

"Already done that," she says. I haul myself out of bed, pull on a pair of sweatpants and a t-shirt, and walk into the bathroom and try the faucet. Nothing. Next, I head downstairs to the kitchen. Eleanor is standing at the sink, attempting to fill the coffee pot with nonexistent water. Mavis says she's going to check and see if Ned has water in the carriage house. Whether the carriage house has running water or not, I need a plumber. And I really hate plumbers. To me, they're the same as auto mechanics. The plumbers understand that barely anyone has plumbing knowledge. The general public is at their mercy. Most of these pipes are underground or under the floorboards, in places no normal person would know to look or want to look. They could tell me anything, like: *There is a giant slug trapped in the main line and we will need to excavate the whole front yard and hire an expert from Alaska.* I promise you, I will believe them and pay them.

"Ms. Green?" says the plumber. He's just come out from under the house wearing a blue plumber's shirt with a 'Charles' decal on the pocket. "It appears someone has removed your pipes."

"Could you please explain that?"

"It's as I said, your pipes are gone. Somebody probably stole them for the copper. Seen it before in an empty house and other buildings, but never in my life on an occupied home."

"What? I've never heard of that. Why would someone do that?"

"Well, ma'am, stories like this have been all over the news, and it's copper, and it's worth something. Unless you have a rich enemy who did this out of spite, I suspect somebody did it for the money."

Enemies? I've never even thought I could have an enemy. Except when I thought the Jersey Guy was stalking me. It was silly of me then to think someone would single me out to harass. So I basically decide that I am not an enemy-prone person and that there must be another explanation.

The plumber tells me PVC is cheaper, and they can start putting some in the kitchen today, so at least we can cook and brush our teeth by tonight. But he says it'll take a while for the rest of the house because their schedule is full. Unfortunately, the carriage house has the same problem. I call around to the other plumbers, but they all tell me they can't even get here for a week. Finally, I get on the phone with a port-o-potty company. I figure we can stick it in the side yard. The guys in the Greek revival will probably have a fit, what with a port-o-let marring their view, but what would they do in the same situation?

"Mavis speakin."

"Hello, I'm calling for Mary Beth Green."

"Who's this?"

"Am I on speaker phone?"

"Maybe…who's this?"

"Bob."

"We don't know no Bob."

"Just give me the phone," I say.

"He sounds slip'ry," says Mavis, handing me the phone.

Mavis loves using speakerphone, but I cut it off.

"This is Mary Beth Green, how may I help you?"

"Mary Beth, I've got great news for you!"

"What might that be?"

"Get ready."

"I'm ready."

"You've won a cruise for three to Bermuda!"

"For three?"

"Yes, three!"

"Three is an awkward number," I say. "What if I only bring one friend?"

"Bring two friends.

"Why can't I bring just one friend?"

"The offer will be void if you only bring one friend."

"This sounds like some kind of trick…to get me and two of my friends trapped on a cruise ship in the middle of the Bermuda Triangle, where we might end up disappearing off the face of the planet. That's too weird for me."

You can't be nice to a telemarketer. It's a fact they'll take advantage of you, and it does not even matter if you tell them just today you had a leg amputated and your mother got run over by a backhoe. They'll try to find a way to make you think that cashing in your retirement for a super-deluxe, one night, two-day stay at a motel with a hot tub is a good deal. So I started this trick in my mind: I tell myself telemarketers are murderers and rapists in prison for life, paying for all their wicked crimes by trying to sell stuff over the phone. This is one of the few times in life it's okay to be rude.

Bob says, "The whole Bermuda Triangle thing is silly. You'll be safe, believe me; it's a promotional cruise."

Bob's voice sounds trusting. Maybe he's in prison for something not so bad, like spray-painting mink coats or check kiting.

16

MARCELLE

I am just about finished getting the house in order for when my sister gets here. Marcelle is five years older and lives in Atlanta. Her favorite activities are working out at Gold's Gym and tweeting. She sells Mary Kay cosmetics for a living and isn't so bad at it. It takes a special type of person to be good at network marketing. She hasn't won herself a pink car yet, but she did win a pink Vespa. She's full of drive. Maybe too much drive, seeing she's driven off two very nice husbands. She lives far enough away for me to breathe easy, seeing that Atlanta is about a five-hour drive. She called me last week, saying she was coming for a visit, but I think she's coming to spy on me and report back to Mother. Since my mother quit drinking, she's become a paragon in her Presbyterian church, and she and Marcelle have been a little more than critical of my Baptist conversion. Especially since it happened when I was living with my father's mother.

Mother once said, "Next thing I know you'll be playing the tambourine in the Winn-Dixie parking lot, selling flowers with the Branch Davidi-ans."

"They're all dead," I told her.

Both Mother and Marcelle are under the impression that Baptists are one step away from being a cult.

I said, "Mother, just because we attend different denominations doesn't mean we don't have the same Jesus." But she thinks her Jesus is more like a member of the British Royal Family—Prince Charles's big brother, eat-ing off Wedgwood with sterling, while my Jesus is the paper plate, baked bean, and snaggletooth one. Mother's Jesus walks around wearing a gold crown with long, blond hair flowing over his shoulders.

One day I am going to write Mother a letter saying Jesus might even be a black man. What if Jesus looked exactly like Don King? Jesus probably was kind of tan, seeing he was Middle Eastern and all. I'm not even sure my mother has any idea our savior is Jewish. This reminds me of the time that Mavis did remember Jesus' ethnic and religious origins two Christ-mases ago. She went to the G.P. and bought a bunch of Manischewitz wine and made matzo ball soup. She said we were gonna celebrate Jesus' birthday the way his own mother would. The soup was delicious, but cheap kosher wine has a distinct flavor, almost identical to grape NyQuil. When we tasted it we all set our glasses down and pretended the moment was too sacred to empty our glasses. One sip made us holy. Mavis served the remains of the kosher wine at Share Group the next night, right next to the iced tea, and Jimmy gulped it down. Anyway, Marcelle should be here soon enough. That means on time for Share Group.

Mavis is wearing a new t-shirt today that reads, *Ass, Grass, or Gas—No One Rides For Free*. I tell her people will make all kinds of assumptions about her based on that shirt.

"I don't mind people thinkin I own me a car," she says.

When the doorbell rings, Mavis goes to answer it. Marcelle's voice immediately echoes through the house, complimenting Mavis, saying how the colors of her shirt set off her eyes. I reach the foot of the steps and say, "Hey, Marcelle. Glad you made it. Do you have any more stuff in the car?"

Marcelle tells me she just has the one bag.

"What happened to your eyebrows?" I ask.

"I went ahead and had them bleached. Don't you think it makes me look like a natural blonde?"

"It looks real natural, all right," says Mavis. "Kinda reminds me of my albino ferret, King Tut. He was a rascal."

"Well, he sounds just adorable," says Marcelle, widening her eyes. Now Marcelle will probably go out and buy herself an albino ferret, so everyone will say how cute they are together—almost like brother and sister.

I lead Marcelle to her room. "Dangit, I almost forgot! Our pipes got stolen."

"Pipes?" she asks. "I was unaware *the Rapturous Rest* owned an organ."

Marcelle thought it was a dumb idea to give the house a name. She said it sounded like I was running a funeral parlor or a brothel. But older siblings can be ugly like that. When I'm eighty and Marcelle is eighty-five, she'll still treat me like I'm three.

"I mean the plumbing. I can't believe I forgot to tell you before you came." I'm kicking myself for forgetting to tell her. She most likely would have stayed home. At least I can guarantee she'll leave soon. "You'll have to brush your teeth in the kitchen. And, so sorry to say, we have a port-o-let set up outside for the rest. As far as bathing goes, you can take a sponge bath, use the shower at the homeless shelter, or check into the Holiday Inn." I turn to go downstairs and say, "Otherwise make yourself at home, and don't feel like you have to join the Share Group if you don't want to. Participation is purely voluntary."

"I wouldn't miss your little meeting for anything," she says.

Mavis and I have the Wednesday supper ready. We've got a rectangle folding table here loaded down with two chicken tetrazzinis, an extra large broccoli-cheese casserole, a salad, and a pile of Hungry Jacks with a tub of I-Can't-Believe-It's-Not-Butter! We've also got three one-gallon jugs of sweet tea, and the drip coffee maker is huffing away. Floyd is staked out under the table.

Terry and Doyle are the first to arrive. They let themselves in and begin pushing the furniture against the walls and pull out the folding chairs for the circle. Then they drift over to the buffet and pick up paper plates.

Terry hasn't really spoken with Doyle since the grocery reading. The situation makes me uncomfortable. What would cause Terry to be so upset that Doyle might spill the beans? People have things they just want to keep private, I guess.

Terry inquires about Marcelle.

"She may or may not come down," I say. I hope she'll take a Valium and stay in her room tonight.

Our usuals are here. We've got Ned, who's no longer boarding in the carriage house. He moved after the pipes got stolen. He found himself a new apartment over the Greek restaurant and says Mr. Stavros, the owner, lets him eat all his meals for free, plus the rent is cheaper. His clothes have become so steeped with the aroma of Greek food that whenever he comes to Share Group, I can't help but think he's got fat wads of moussaka or souvlaki stuffed in his pockets.

Jimmy shows up with some of his employees, or under painters. They're looking a little hangdog tonight, but then again they always look that way when Jimmy makes them come to Share Group. Jimmy's under the impression that if they can open up and share together, they will have a stronger painting team. It was my idea, really. I said, "Jimmy, instead of taking those boys out drinking and carousing after work, why don't you bring them here to relax and get some things off their hearts and minds?" Jimmy's two employees are Phil and Baby George. They're both in their twenties.

"Hello there, Baby George," I say.

"Ma'am," says Baby George.

"It's nice to see you, Phil."

Phil nods. He looks a little like Gary Busey, if he were a house painter.

We sit around with paper plates, chatting and eating until seven; then we cover all the food and start getting settled for Share Group.

About that time, Eleanor walks in with a bundle of shopping bags and heads for the stairs. She bumps into Marcelle, who's on her way down, wearing perfectly ironed jeans, a low-cut blouse, and shiny black flats. I wish she'd change that blouse.

"Oh, my Lord!" shouts Marcelle. "That's a Dundy's bag!"

"Yes it is," says Eleanor. "I was just there and bought up half the store."

Marcelle says, "Our grandmother used to take me and Mary Beth there every summer. As soon as we'd arrive in Brightleaf, we'd head straight to Dundy's for new swimsuits and sundresses. Mr. Dundy had this huge bowl of candy on a table in the middle of the store. I loved that candy bowl. Mary Beth was never allowed to have any. She always did have to watch her weight—"

"Marcelle, I was allowed candy."

But Marcelle ignores me, saying, "Just look at *you*!" Marcelle motions to Eleanor, who is a real-life anorexic. "Don't you have a cute little figure?"

Don't tell her she's got a cute figure, I think to myself. *We'll have to go ahead and make funeral arrangements if she gets any cuter.*

"Marcelle!" I say her name loudly to make her clam up. "I'm glad you came down. Come and join the circle if you want."

Winslow arrives. He apparently jogged to Share Group again. He's wearing a sleeveless t-shirt, which doesn't do much for his stringy arms (we all can see his gray, frizzy underarm hair poking out), with long patches of sweat soaking his back, chest, underarms, and some nasty patches below the waist. Winslow immediately notices Marcelle and makes a beeline for her, taking the opportunity to extend a warm welcome to a new female. He takes both her hands in his and says, "You are just as gorgeous as your sister."

"Thank…you." Marcelle is visibly taken aback by Winslow, but she snaps out of it real quick and says, "You know, you've got one of the longest ponytails I've ever seen on a man." She politely pulls away from his grip and wipes her hands off on the sides of her jeans.

"Thank you, my dear," he says, stroking his hair.

Marcelle finds a chair, and Winslow picks the one next to it.

"May I offer you a cigarette?" Winslow asks, shamelessly scooching over until their chairs touch.

"No, thank you. I've quit."

Marcelle has been smoking on the sly since she was twelve. Most people didn't even know. I doubt our mother even knows.

"All right," I say. "Time to prepare our hearts and minds to share. For those who are new to Share Group, please remember to keep your hands to yourselves, no laughing at anyone or insults allowed." Baby George and Phil begin making obscene gestures at one another like they're fixing to break the rules.

I glance at Marcelle, but she isn't listening because she's so distracted by Winslow, who's resting his arm on the back of her chair, giving us a gaping view of his underarm, like a giant tarantula wet from a swim. Marcelle is doing everything in her power to prevent that drippy underarm hair from touching her blouse. Even though Winslow is totally breaking the rules, I pretend I don't notice. I look at my wall scripture about the strangers maybe being angels. There are no strangers here tonight. We begin.

"Mary Beth done won a cruise to the Bermuda Triangle," says Mavis.

That was my news. And I hadn't planned on telling anyone just yet.

"She gets to take two friends," says Mavis.

"I still need to look into it and find out what the catch is, so nobody go getting your hopes up," I say.

Baby George says, "We should all draw straws to see who the lucky two will be!"

"Baby George, I'm not taking any men." I imagine the possible combination of Baby George and Winslow as travel companions. Wilting.

Ned says, "Man, I had another dream. You guys wanna hear it?"

We all nod.

"I'm warning you," he says, "it's gonna blow your freakin' minds."

"Still keeping the dream journal?" asks Winslow.

"I totally wrote it all down," says Ned. "Anyways, the other morning I woke to the voice of the Fonz calling me. *Ned, Ned,* he called. I said, *Fonz? Is that you? Why are you in my dream, man?* And then the Fonz says, *I'm gonna save you from Evil Otto, Ned. Here, take my jukebox and ride like lightening!* It made sense to me in the dream that the jukebox doubles as a motorcycle. So I'm getting ready to jump on the jukebox, but as I turn around, Evil Otto is right behind me, shouting, *Chicken!* Then I hear the voice of the Fonz again, but it's not coming from the Fonz's mouth but from somewhere outside, so I sit up in bed to look outside, and that's when I see the TV is on. And I realize I'm awake and watching a *Happy Days* rerun. What do you guys think?"

"Which episode?" asks Jimmy.

"It was the one where the Fonz takes off his leather jacket and quits being cool for a while. It had definite significance."

"Did you fall asleep with the TV on?" I ask.

"I turned it off, and I'm totally sure because I was watching *Blade*, and the end was coming where it gets totally freaky, and everybody starts getting vampiry. And that guy turns into the devil, you know? And my finger was shaking on the remote because it was so scary, I couldn't turn the TV off fast enough."

Ned is an intelligent guy, and we already discovered he has skills no one would suspect, so he probably knows more than we suspect. He could probably beat all of us here at Trivial Pursuit, which would make him practically a genius in my book, but he watches way too much television to lead a normal life. His forehead is beading up, like he just relived it all.

81

I'm glad he got that off his chest. That's why we share.

Phil says, "Speaking of scary, I think my truck is haunted."

Terry says, "Like the car, Christine?"

"Haunted. Not *possessed*," says Phil, shaking his head like we should all know the difference.

"Sorry," says Terry. "But what's the difference?"

"Possessed is when a person or a thing gets a evil spirit living inside it. Haunted is when a place has ghosts. Ghosts are people, and evil spirits are not people. Understand? So like I was saying, I'm pretty sure my truck is haunted."

Phil looks extremely serious, but Terry is evidently entertained and says, "Tell us why you think your truck has a ghost, then."

Phil's eyes get wide, and he says in almost a whisper, "Stuff is always disappearing from my truck. Then, other stuff that isn't mine shows up outta the blue. And I'm almost too afraid to drive it at times. I go out to the truck, and there is all this crap I've never seen before in my life!"

"Like what?" asks Eleanor.

"Stuff like potted plants, mailboxes, and lawn chairs."

Eleanor wrinkles her nose and says, "You think a ghost put those there?"

Phil slowly nods and says, "How else do you explain it?"

"Does that stuff ever appear after a hard night of drinking, Phil?" asks Winslow.

Then Baby George pipes up saying he knows where the Confederate Gold is buried, but Jimmy gives him the evil eye and elbows him in the ribs.

Marcelle is fidgeting in her chair like she'd like to speak. She clears her throat and stands up – a thing we don't normally do in Share Group, stand up – and says, "I'm a smoker."

Oh brother.

"Marcelle, sit down. This is not a Smokers Anonymous meeting," I say.

"She may feel more comfortable standing," says Terry. He's sitting next to me with his arms crossed, kind of leaning back in his chair. "Isn't that the gist of Share Group?" He looks my way.

"Go ahead, then," I say because Marcelle won't sit down. She just wants to be the center of attention.

"I've now been smoke-free for one month. Because I met the healer!"

"The healer, huh?" I say.

"His name is Lonnie Jr. And he's a Christian hypnotist."

"Is that like a Christian Scientist?" asks Eleanor.

"Wait a minute," I say. "The person who accuses Baptists and Catholics of being in *alternative* religions thinks hypnotists are okay?"

"Mary Beth, babe," says Mavis, wrinkling her forehead. "You're breakin your own rules talkin that way."

"He's for real," says Marcelle. "That's why I came. To testify! Lonnie Jr. can heal you of anything. And fix all your problems! He's also so charming and charismatic. You're gonna love him."

"Okay. That's great. Thanks for testifying. You may sit down now."

Marcelle is still standing there like I just told her to please stand as much as she wants. Terry looks perplexed, and Mavis looks thoughtful.

"We're gonna love him?" asks Mavis. "He's comin to the Rapturous Rest?"

Marcelle nods with a big smile. "Next week!"

Mavis claps her hands and says, "Goody! If he's as magical as you says he is, I know somebody who needs a taste of his medicine."

"Great idea," says Terry. "A guest speaker."

"I didn't invite him," I say. Grocery store psychics, hypnotists…what's next? Snake charmers and necromancers?

Marcelle says, "I did you a favor, Miss Mary Beth." A few people laugh.

Mavis should donate her *I'm the BIG Sister* shirt to Marcelle.

"You can thank me later."

To keep from charging Marcelle, knocking her flat on the floor, and slapping her silly like a middle school gang girl, I say, "Would ya'll excuse me, please?" I hold my hand to my head and tell them I think it's a migraine.

I'm sitting on the bed in my grandmother's old room. Mazie Lee Green lived a full life until five years ago, when she had a heart attack working in her garden. A friend found her lying peacefully in a bed of lavender, embracing an armload of dahlias. She was 89. I feel her spirit here more than any place in the house. The wallpaper is the same pearly pink with the white print of flower-filled urns, peeling at the seams. The woodwork—doors, windows and crown molding—is still the same high-gloss white. Voices from downstairs float up, but I can't make out what anyone is saying. Occasionally a few people laugh. Maybe Marcelle is entertaining them with stories from our childhood, like when I was six and I tried to fly. I climbed up a twelve-foot ladder and jumped off, flapping my arms. I pull out one of my grandmother's Perry Como albums, *The Golden Records*, and set it on the turntable. I position the needle to "Catch A Falling Star," turn down the volume to barely audible, and pick up the *People* magazine on my nightstand, slowly turning the pages.

Catch a falling star and put it in your pocket, save it for a rainy day, sings Perry.

When I first moved back into the house, five months after my grandmother passed, the scent of her talcum powder still lingered powerfully. It's faint now, but I believe it will always be here, or at least I will expect it to be, so it will. The white chenille bedspread is fraying but passes for shabby chic. The windows face the street, so if I wanted to I could know everything that's going on in my front yard, across the street, and halfway down the hill. Not only is it my grandmother's room – maybe because of it – whenever I enter, I feel like I'm moving into a dimension separate from the other parts of the house. It's a pocket of cleaner air, made up of whatever type of atoms are used in creating the substance of congruence and the properties of rest. One reason why I named the house what I did. I almost feel like I'm in an episode of *Star Trek*, when Captain Kirk steps into a new world. Something shifts for me in here.

For love may come and tap you on your shoulder some starless night,
Just in case you think you want to hold her,
You'll have a pocket full of starlight…

I regroup and kick myself for letting my sister get the best of me, for reacting to her like I did as a child. I sit here listening to the sounds of the evening unwind downstairs. Voices grow fainter until they disappear down the street or behind car doors. Outside, trashcan lids slam, metal to metal, signaling some good soul taking out the last of the day's trash. I pick up the arm of the record player and set the needle to "Papa Likes Mambo." I'm waiting for everyone to clear out, so I can sneak down to the kitchen with my toothbrush and use the port-o-let. About fifteen minutes ago, I heard Marcelle tell Mavis goodnight, so I figure the coast is probably clear.

I push my door open and see the light of the TV below, though no one is watching. As I move through the living room, there's a knock on the front door. I peek through the peephole. It's Terry Dorrie.

I crack the door.

"You weren't asleep, were you?" he asks.

I shake my head. "I just came down to brush my teeth."

"Oh, good. I think I left my briefcase."

I open the door all the way and tell him he's welcome to come in and look around.

He steps over the threshold, walks into the great room and clear around the sofa.

"Mind if I turn on a lamp?" he asks. He looks behind the wingback chairs and in the hall closet. "I may have left it in the kitchen."

During the day, the kitchen is bright and caffeinated, but now the fluorescent light over the stove reflects off the canary yellow walls, converting them to a soft gold, blanketing the room with warmth and stillness. The briefcase is sitting on the floor, leaning against the leg of a kitchen chair.

"I'm really sorry to bother you when you're getting ready for bed," he says, reaching for his briefcase. "But I'm happy to see you." He stands up and looks at me with an expression that's difficult to define.

"Thanks," I say, crossing my arms over my robe, clutching my toothbrush. I'm self-conscious about my old robe and hope Dr. Dorrie doesn't feel like he needs to make small talk. "Well, glad you found your briefcase," I say. "I'd walk you to the door, but I'm a mess."

He stands there looking at me. "Gotta minute?" he asks.

I shrug.

"I feel like I owe you an apology for taking sides with your sister tonight. It wasn't intentional. At the time I didn't realize how much it would bother you."

I nod, grateful to hear him say that.

"But I can't help feeling that I've offended you before tonight somehow."

"Why's that?" I say.

"Because you never talk to me."

"We're talking now." I give him a half smile, trying my best to be polite.

"Yeah, but that's not what I mean. Did I say something at my office that put you off? Or was it at the traffic light when I told you your brake lights were out?"

"I was really happy you told me about that. I'd probably be dead, if you didn't."

"Okay. It just feels like you avoid me on purpose. Maybe that sounds strange."

I wish I could tell this nice man that it was not him that did anything. It was me. Instead I say with a forced laugh, "I guess I've been really distracted lately. My life is crazy!"

"Okay," he says. "I get that." He gives me a nod, picks up his briefcase and starts for the door.

I set my toothbrush on the counter. I don't want to have long conversations with Terry Dorrie and end up slowly becoming good friends with him and really *liking* the man whose dog I stole. On the other hand, I recognize I'm not treating him like I would anybody else. I'm normally friendly with everyone I meet (with a few exceptions), so with as much grace as I can muster, I say, "Can I do anything for you, Terry? Do you need something?"

He stops in the kitchen door and looks at me. He says, "What can you do for me? I'm not so needy that I need you to do anything for me. I just thought we could talk."

"About what?"

"Anything. Maybe we could have dinner Friday, Saturday?"

"Like...a date?" I can't decide if Terry Dorrie feels sorry for me or is asking me on a date. It would be pretty strange to go on a date with the Jersey Guy. My sort-of gynecologist. He needs to quit thinking he hurt my feelings so bad at Share Group tonight.

"Whatever you want it to be," he says. "We can hang out outside of the group here."

I sincerely disdain dating. I say, "I don't think I can. I've got a church fellowship meeting on Friday, and I've already committed to bringing the beef stroganoff. And Saturdays are for book-keeping, meal-planning and shopping, which pretty much whips me for the rest of the weekend." Which is all the truth.

"I like stroganoff," he says.

"You'd get bored. You won't know a soul there," I say.

"I'll know you."

"Where do you normally go to church, anyway?"

"I'm Catholic but haven't been to a Mass in ages. In fact, I probably need to do something churchy so the guy in the sky doesn't forget about me," he says with a smile.

He's not giving up. So I say, "Ok, but be ready when I pick you up."

"Great!" he says.

When I ask Terry for directions to his house to pick him up, I feel guilty for pretending not to know where he lives. But the drive over to the church isn't too terrible. Terry asks where I grew up and about my family. He asks me where I went to college and what my major was. I tell him Chapel Hill with a degree in Education, and that I taught kindergarten for six years in Greensboro before moving back to Brightleaf to help my grandmother the last few years of her life.

When Terry insists I find a teaching job in Brightleaf, I tell him that I love the children, but it wasn't easy. Teachers have to be like superheroes: they go around doing great feats and get a lot of criticism.

"What about boyfriends, or dare I say...marriage?" Terry asks.

"Nada."

"I don't believe it."

"Too busy. Well, I had a kind of boyfriend once. And it seemed like we were starting something, until he went to London to work on a graduate degree and I never heard from him again."

"I'm sorry."

An uneasy silence fills my car until Terry speaks up again.

"Where's the steeple?" He starts laughing when he sees my church building.

"There's no rule that a church needs a steeple," I say as we pull into the parking lot of a defunct Wendy's. Jesus never said he'd be wherever there are two or more steeples gathered in his name.

In my mind, a Wendy's makes a perfect church. You've got a big kitchen and a long counter to use as a buffet. Then all that good seating. I like the way we don't all sit in straight rows and look straight ahead at the preacher. The regular Wendy's tables and chairs are a nice change from conventional pews.

The stroganoff is in a Pyrex dish covered with foil. Terry walks it over to the buffet and squeezes it between two plates of deviled eggs, evidently brought by two different people. The food at potlucks always gives you a real feel for the person who made it. I don't make judgments about people and their food in the same way I do with front yards and statuary. But it does show you little things, like obviously who can cook and who can't, and who enjoys paying attention to small details and…who cannot get enough of the flavor Amaretto.

I sit at a table with the Henricos, an older couple who've been coming here for longer than me. Dot Henrico just came down with Bell's palsy, and her face is half paralyzed. Her husband, Bill, is telling me the details and about the doctor visits. Dot just nods and smiles with the half of her face that still works. I am impressed that she is in such good spirits, under the circumstances. Terry should be back from dropping off the stroganoff, but he's walking around the room and shaking hands with different people. Out of the corner of my eye, I see him point over to where I am, and each person turns to me and smiles. Then he walks up to Deacon Coons and his wife, Belinda. They give one another big hugs, and he kisses Belinda on the cheek. Bill Henrico is still telling me about Dot's doctor visits, and I don't want to be rude to these nice people, so I keep on listening and having the concerned look and nodding, all the while keeping an eye on Terry and the Coons, who are over there just yacking it up, apparently having some kind of reunion. Terry is talking and gesturing with his hands, and Deacon Coons and Belinda are laughing like they think Terry is a regular Jerry Seinfeld. Belinda gives him a playful push on he arm like she's saying, *Terry Dorrie, you just kill me!*

Terry never tells me funny stories. Now, I want to sprint over there and find out what's so dang hilarious and how Terry knows my church deacon and his wife. But Bill Henrico is really rolling with the Bell's palsy story, so I have no choice but to hear it to the end.

The room hums so loudly with the chatter of friends catching up that we barely hear the bell ring. It rings again, and everyone begins to quiet down and find their seats. The minister says a prayer, blessing the food (Potluck food needs extra blessing in my opinion. Just think: you have no clue who made it, how long its been sitting out, or if somebody sneezed on it.), prays for Dot Henrico's speedy recovery, and ends with something like, *help us fight the good fight against gluttony.* After the prayer, Terry makes his way to our table, where I introduce him to the Henricos. They shake hands, and Bill says, "Hey Terry, why don't we all hit the buffet, then I'll fill you in on what I was just telling Mary Beth. Boy, we've had a time with the doctors."

As we walk to the buffet, I say, "I see you know Deacon Coons and his wife."

Terry says, "Tip and Belinda? Great running into them. Really nice people."

At the buffet, Belinda comes up, squeezes my arm, and whispers, "I didn't know that you and Terry were seeing eachother! He's such a great gynecologist, don't you think? *Great catch!*"

I about drop my plate.

For the remainder of the evening, Terry is seriously engrossed in the story of Dot Henrico's Bell's palsy. He wants to know who all her doctors are, the procedures, the prognosis, etc. I thought Terry would be at a loss here, but he's right at home. *Great catch?* I wasn't fishing. He just kind of jumped into my net.

17

A CULTURAL DAY

July 4, 1990

Dear Diary,

I woke up today thinking, Fourth of July! The middle of summer! No work! I snuggled under the covers, hoping to go back to sleep until noon. But right away old Mazie knocked on my door and told me I was coming with her to the soup kitchen. I was super scared. Not sure why, but maybe I thought I'd see a bunch of scary beggars with no teeth, talking to themselves. I don't know. There were some scary beggars with no teeth but also a few tired-looking moms with little kids. There were a couple of men with brushed hair, shaved faces and had their shirts tucked in. One guy looked a little bit like my daddy. It wasn't him, of course. First of all, my daddy's face never gets that tan, and he's a lawyer in Savannah. Plus, he would not hang out at the soup kitchen in Brightleaf but go directly to

Grandmother's house. So today I helped serve food. Harriet, the lady in charge, said that a restaurant dropped off a bunch of sausages and rice, so she made dirty rice and opened up a gigantic can of peaches to serve on the side. Suddenly, I was starving for peaches and dirty rice. All of a sudden it seemed like the best meal in the world. Harriet said it was because I couldn't have any. It wasn't for me. We want what we can't have. Then Harriet talked about getting creative with the food donations, which seemed fun. Like art class. She told me one time all they had were mushrooms and kidney beans. Every day for a week Harriet made mushroom soup, kidney bean and mushroom curry, and mushroom caps stuffed with kidney bean paste. All the homeless vegetarians must have been thrilled. I told her that I would like to help cook sometime.

Baptists aren't totally retarded...X

18

LONNIE JR. THE HEALER

Mavis

I'm thinkin that I might-could get Manchild some help from Marcelle's healer-man. Manchild needs all the help he can get nowadays…even if he gets put in a trance to brush his teeth more regular. All I know is that since I done shooed him off and Eleanor done got sick of him tryin to romance her, he's been actin like a stinker. He's already gone to jail for muggin a pregnant girl. Then he got picked up by the police for hangin around the schoolyard and followin youngsters with his hands wagglin down his britches. His eyes done gone from beady to mean. So if there's anybody out there passin out miracles, Manchild needs to break in line and get him one.

Mary Beth

Lonnie Jr. the Healer is a lot shorter than I thought he'd be. For some reason, when Marcelle said she met the healer, I imagined him with a long beard and staff, kind of like Swami Ken meets Billy Graham, but instead he's more like Yoda meets Liberace. Lonnie Jr.'s got a head of thick, black hair sculpted stiff with gel and bulgy, blue eyes. He's also got a teeny goatee, and his side burns are trimmed into right angles. He looks pretty hypnotist-like. Why not fit the part? He's wearing an electric blue silk shirt and a heavy gold chain around his neck with a fat medallion hanging from it. I bet that's what he swings to make people obey. I won't look at it. He's not putting any spells on me.

I'm hiding Floyd, too. I once read in *Woman's World* that hypnotized pets are demanding. Always wanting to shake a paw, and prancing around on hind legs.

Lonnie Jr. walks directly to me. I fight the temptation to snatch a glimpse at the gold coin moored around his neck. I feel it shining in the corner of my eye and sense its magical pull. I could be imagining the magical pull.

"Hello," he says softly. "May I?"

Before I get the chance to say, *No*, he reaches out his arms, grabs my face, and cradles my chin and cheeks in both of his hands. This is a new experience, and I kind of like it, except for the fact that he is probably trying to hypnotize me.

I don't know if I should close my eyes or keep them open, so I close them in a duel effort to resist the medallion and avoid eye contact. His hands are warm, and I feel my jaw and shoulders relax.

"You have a lot of tension. I noticed the moment I saw you," says Lonnie Jr.

I want to say something, but my face is so relaxed I can't speak. My cheeks feel rubberized, like Novocain dead.

The numbness flows through my nervous system, and at the same time it feels like a whole flood of clean water is rushing through me. Only it's warm water. But more like sunshine, and...

"He did that to me, too," says Marcelle. "Lonnie Jr., this is Mary Beth.

My sister."

"Mary Beth," says Lonnie Jr., now taking both of my hands in his, "It's a pleasure."

I gulp. I was seriously having an experience. I was seeing the Light. I was about to break on through to the other side. Marcelle steps back a few feet, so Lonnie Jr. and everyone can get a good look at her in her tarty dress.

"Lonnie Jr.," says Marcelle, practically gushing, "I'm smoke-free, thanks to you and your healing ways. Look at me!" She runs her hands down her sides. "I jog without coughing, and my road rage is under control. It's been two months since I ran a bicyclist off the road. Can you help these people, Lonnie Jr.? Especially my sister, Mary Beth? I know you can give her the power she needs to shed those unwanted pounds. They might start calling you the Hypno-Slimmer!"

I look down at my body. One more workout with Richard Simmons each week wouldn't hurt.

"Mary Beth is beautiful the way she is," says Terry. "Although if he is a hypno-slimmer I might be interested in his services down the road." He smiles, patting his flat stomach. "But we also hoped Lonnie Jr. could help a friend of Mavis's. A very disturbed young man."

Marcelle puts a smile on and says, "Of course!" But I sense her freedom from road rage being challenged.

Winslow slides over to Marcelle to comfort her. He puts his hand on her waist and says in a low voice, "I need help...but I doubt the hypnotist has a cure for what ails me." Marcelle looks uncomfortable with Winslow's hand on her.

Manchild finally shows up. He scuffles in wearing brown corduroys worn through at the knees and on his backside, so it's whitish in those places. He's got on an old tuxedo shirt with yellow stains. I welcome him, but he ignores me, which is good. Nobody needs scary people paying attention to them. Mavis was right: Manchild looks meaner than before. Eleanor rushes over to him and tries to hug him.

Lickety-split he grabs her wrist and says, "Don't you touch me, you strang bean of a woman."

Eleanor had a plan to get Manchild honest work by helping him become a gardener. She bought him a leaf blower, a weed whacker and a pair of loppers. It was a wonder anyone hired him since he looks so seamy, but some people will give anyone a chance. And I love that. Unfortunately, Manchild tore up the yard of each and every customer. He didn't have an eye for sculpting shrubs. When one man refused to pay him for destroying his shrubbery, Manchild chased him with the weed whacker until an officer showed up. Then Eleanor had a revelation that Manchild needed to release his creative side, so she bought him a camera. He did not pass Go with the camera but took it directly to the pawnshop. Now he's telling Eleanor he wants to become a professional golfer. He says that when he was in jail he watched the Player's Championship on TV, and it was very inspirational. He's positive he would look great in a pink golf shirt and green pants and would love the chance to smack a ball for easy cash.

Eleanor seems unruffled, despite the fact that Manchild could easily snap her hand off. "Manchild, if you'd allow yourself to get a little help, I might buy those golf clubs for you," she says.

"What I got to do?" asks Manchild, squinting at everyone.

Mavis says, "Manchild, baby, I know you ain't much on religion, but here's somebody calls hisself a hypnotist for Jesus. Just hope you'll let him say a little prayer over you."

"As long as he don't try to cast out no devils. I already had that. And I get me a golf cart, too." He looks at Eleanor.

For Pete's sake. They need to let Manchild go. He's plainly a mental case and would benefit from a little shock therapy or something. And when I think he may own the keys to a golf cart soon…

I look around the room at my friends. They're still and solemn and look genuinely expectant. Even both of Doyle's eyes are at peace for a moment. I am struck by how much these people care about Manchild.

How many people would go out of their way to help an angry deviant? Create a plan to lure him into a trap where he could get help? Even though the "help" part remains to be seen.

"Here, you want me to hold your hand, baby?" asks Mavis.

Manchild shrugs and sort of makes a little motion towards Mavis.

"That's right," whispers Mavis. "It'll be all right." She squeezes his hand.

"Okay," says Lonnie Jr., standing in front of them like he's about to marry them. "Focus on the coin around my neck."

I knew it.

"Now, Manchild, I'm going to place my hands on your face and speak some words into you. Are you okay with that?"

Manchild nods, but he looks at Lonnie Jr. the Healer like he'd rather eat him.

"Keep your eyes on the coin," says Lonnie Jr., oblivious to Manchild's cannibalistic stare.

Terry looks back at me and smiles. I do half a smile.

Lonnie Jr. says, "In the beginning God made you good, Manchild. Now, I'm taking you back. Back before you ever did any wrong...I see you as a baby. Yes. You are a baby lying on a dirty blanket with an empty bottle in your hand. You've been wearing the same diaper for days. You don't know you're neglected. You don't know your mother is either drunk or passed out all day. You don't know your father has abandoned you. You don't understand the abuses of life yet. You are hungry, and you have a painful diaper rash, but you still trust. You trust everything is going to be okay. You are good and know nothing but goodness and love. Be there right now with me. In that hidden place you once knew. The place where goodness and trust and love abide. And now, feel the love. Feel the love flowing from my hands."

I don't know what to think right now. This Lonnie Jr., he is saying the things I always suspected about people. The things about babies being good and trusting but being served up a plate of rottenness they accept, believing for the best. Not realizing they are being poisoned for the rest of their lives. A spiritual salmonella, taking root in their hopeful hearts.

Manchild's shoulders slacken. His head tilts towards Mavis until it's resting against hers. The hand he's clutching Mavis with loosens. I cannot see his face from where I'm sitting, but I'd bet you all the gold medallions in Atlantic City he's drooling.

Lonnie Jr. claps his hands hard in front of Manchild's face. Manchild jumps before falling backwards. His head hits the floor with a thud. He doesn't move.

"My god," says Terry, jumping out of his chair. He kneels beside Manchild and asks him some questions. Manchild doesn't speak. Terry checks his pulse. He lifts Manchild's eyelid and tells Winslow to call an ambulance.

Lonnie Jr. appears to be unconcerned and nonchalant about the ambulance being called. This angers me. I march over to him, figuring I could maybe strangle him with his necklace, and then notice that Mavis is in some sort of trance. If I weren't so troubled by this development, I'd rush upstairs for my camera. She's motionless but with a queer look in her eyes, like she's on one of those space shows and a paralyzer gun zapped her good. I'm pretty sure she'd want a picture of herself.

"What's wrong with Mavis?" I ask Lonnie Jr.

"There must have been some power overflow." He looks pleased with himself.

"Bring her back, this instant." I feel like Samantha from *Bewitched*, yelling at Endora to turn Darren back from a donkey to a person again.

He claps, and Mavis yawns.

"Mavis, are you okay?"

"Sure, babe. Good to go. Where's Manchild?"

It's dark. I stumble in from the port-o-let, haul myself up the steps, and climb into bed. I slide between cool sheets and pull the covers up to my chin. Manchild is safe in a hospital and Mavis free from her trance. A

98

streetlamp shines through the blinds, making stripes on the ceiling. I stare at those glowing lines, finding it hard to sleep after the evening's excitement. My cheeks are tingling. I can still feel Lonnie Jr.'s hands on them, warm and dry. The heat goes down inside of me, through my face, down into my neck and stomach and legs, melting me to sleep. I'm riding in a car with Lonnie Jr., his medallion shining in the sun. He tells me to fasten my seatbelt, so we can escape. Escape from what? The Lexus. I turn around in my seat, and there's Terry Dorrie, driving like a madman behind us. He wants to catch us.

19

AFTER EFFECTS

Mavis

An inneresting thing did happen in the car when me and Winslow followed the ambulance carrying Manchild. He done pulled out his pack of Basics and tossed one my way. Normally, I ain't one to turn down nothin free. But when I picked up that cigarette, I had no more desire to smoke it than an old tampon.

I says, "Winslow babe, it kinda seems like I been hit by the trance of quittin. And I ain't sayin I'm particularly happy about it, neither. I hate gettin hit with shit I ain't asked for."

Winslow kept his eyes on the road, shrugged his shoulders, and held out his hand for the Basic. He stuffed it back in his shirt pocket.

"Let me know if you change your mind," he says.

Mary Beth

The hypnotist is not anyone I'd go out with, even if he did become a famous hypno-slimmer. I'm ashamed I let myself be charmed by the medallion and his hands on my face. I must be a desperate soul to dream about someone who looks like a magical mobster.

I like being single. I don't ever think about being in touch with my sexual side, like *Redbook* always talks about. Still, I've never felt the way I did when Lonnie Jr. put his hands on me.

I'm sitting at breakfast when Marcelle walks in the house, fresh from the port-o-let, wearing a jogging bra and athletic shorts. She says she's checking out.

"I can't stay here one more day," she says. "I must bathe, unlike the rest of you. Plus, my time here has been somewhat profitable. I did what I came to do."

"You might as well just go on ahead and say, *It is finished*," I tell Marcelle, referencing Jesus Christ, himself. Marcelle thinks she's real smart coming in here and fixing everything. If you consider Manchild getting a concussion and Mavis being forced to quit smoking against her will as fixing everything. I'm tidying up the living room in case any down-and-outers wander in today for a relaxing rerun of *90210*. Going without a shower for a day or two doesn't bother me.

"It *is* finished—except for that little bit of weight you've got to work on," says Marcelle, poking my side and smiling. Then she heads upstairs to pack.

I've been persecuted by a couple of Presbyterians my whole life long.

"I always thought you and your cigarettes would be buried together," I tell Mavis.

"Yep. I kinda had the same idea. I'd be all laid out, wearin my favorite t-shirt, with rouge on my cheeks, and maybe some fake tanner. My hair would be feathered on one side, with a banana clip holding back the other side. Then I'd have me a cigarette wedged between my lips in a thoughtful way, not lit of course, just for show. I'd be a sight to behold! It'd be the last time anybody sees me in the flesh. And the men, when the men sees me all laid out that way, they'll hold their hearts."

"There's something seriously wrong with that," I say.

"My cousin Livira looked that good. You shoulda been there to hear some of the things folks said. There ain't nothin wrong with puttin your best foot forward. Even if your best foot is a dead foot."

The doorbell rings, and Mavis answers it.

"Flowers!" yells Mavis from the foyer. "Somebody done sent you some flowers, girl!" She walks into the kitchen carrying a long pink box filled with Stargazers. "Mmm, they smell like PER-fume. I done told you. You need to give Doc more attention. He's hot for you, baby. Looka here, the card says, *Dear Beautiful Mary Beth, Something about you touched something in me last night. You swing? 912-555-6809.*"

"You think Terry sent that? Swing? I'm a little big for playgrounds. What about that phone number? That is not Terry's."

Mavis has the phone in her hand. She's shaking her head while she dials. "Generally speakin, swang don't mean the playground, darlin."

When someone on the other end answers, she says, "Hey baby! I got them flowers! They're so purdy. Hm? No, this is Mavis. Who's this? You didn't sign your name. Who? You think I've got the wrong what? I'd be glad to come on over this minute. Oh really? Well okay, tough luck, baby, but I really love them lilies. Bye, now."

"Well?" I ask when she hangs up.

"I give you one guess, and it ain't Doc."

I feel myself blushing. I don't want to say, but I know.

"It was the scalawag who dropped the hammer on my smokes."

Mavis, Eleanor and I are in the kitchen washing the last of the serving spoons after a regular boarding house breakfast of scrambled eggs, biscuits, and fruit.

Mavis has on a tube top and blue jeans today, which surprisingly makes her look young and spritely, and her hair is all done up in a banana clip. Eleanor is pacing around glumly in a designer t-shirt that hangs off her bony shoulders. Eleanor's spiky black hair has grown past her eyes. She's clearly not herself these days. Not that Eleanor is ever the life of the party, but she normally navigates her day in some variation of high-strung mode, liberally passing out critiques or terse comments. Someone you'd like to see slow down, eat a bowl of mashed potatoes, and take a long nap. I'd like to see her eat, period. But I gotta say it's no fun seeing her this way. It's like Eleanor's weighed down by some invisible load.

"Eleanor, you okay, darlin'?"

"Actually I'm not. It took you long enough to notice."

"I've noticed you haven't been yourself for a few days now."

"Well, you didn't ask. Also, I haven't heard you ask about Ned."

"I thought about Ned the other night," I tell Eleanor. "I noticed he hasn't been around all that much since he moved."

"Why don't you call him?"

"I'm not going to keep leaving voicemails."

It wouldn't surprise me if Ned's voicemail box is filled with messages from a bunch of girls worrying about him. Guys like Ned end up with lots of saviors.

"Speaking of people going MIA, anybody seen Manchild since the other night? Did anyone check on him the day he got released from the hospital?"

Mavis and Eleanor both give me guilty looks.

"Look, baby," says Mavis. "I feel sorry for Manchild and all, but once you shake off a rattle snake, you run like hell and don't look back. I took a risk invitin him over to get help from that healer man, but I don't want him in my life. At all."

"I probably should have checked on him," I say, "but I was out of it after all that hocus pocus business."

Mavis says, "Eleanor cut him off for good. So maybe he done run off."

Eleanor nods and says, "But I promised him golf clubs if he let Lonnie

Jr. hypnotize him. I'm surprised he hasn't come by to collect."

"Me, too," I say. "But somebody should make sure he's not locked up in some psychiatric ward, or stumbling around with amnesia."

"A psycho ward ain't a bad place if you need it," says Mavis.

That's the truth. I feel like Manchild was probably better off before Lonnie Jr. got his hands on him.

I hate it that Lonnie Jr. had such power over all of us. And it's disgusting how he made us feel like he had some kind of love in him. Then the very next day he sends me that sleazy card asking if I'm a swinger. Gross. I let my imagination go for just a minute. I see myself trapped in a room with him. He's wearing the medallion and no shirt. And he's running at me with his hands outstretched like he wants to lay them on my face again and stun me like a jellyfish.

"I still don't get it how somebody so shallow can have that kind of power," I say.

"Hey, baby, I ain't gonna fight over whether or not the troll was pure in heart, but the fact stands that I still can't put a cigarette to my lips. That took somethin powerful."

20

IT'S A DATE

Mavis

"Mavis speakin," I says into the phone.

"Mavis, it's Terry. How are ya?"

"Hangin in there, Doc. How bout yourself?"

"Good...I'm good. Actually, I'm calling to ask a favor."

"Ask away, darlin."

"I have this function coming up. It's nothing big. But it's important to me. Would you be up for going with me?"

"You askin me on a date, Doc? I unnerstand how I'm attractive to younger men and all, but don't you think Mary Beth is the lady you should ask?"

"Well..."

"Ya'll both know why you hang around the house all the time."

"Mary Beth is a difficult woman to understand...and some of my hobbies may not sit well with her. She distrusts me for some reason. How can you get close to someone who doesn't trust you?"

"By talkin to 'em. But don't feel bad, darlin. Mary Beth don't trust most men who try and get friendly with her."

"That's why I need you to come with me. I need your opinion on how to proceed with Mary Beth regarding this thing I do."

"Darlin, there is so many more fish in your sea. I don't recommend wastin your time with her. Just sayin. I like you too much to let your heart go gettin broken."

"I like a challenge."

"Don't say I didn't warn you. But I could use some excitement. You got me, baby."

21

THE HUEY INCIDENT CONTINUES

July 20, 1990

Dear Diary,

Today was apparently a big day for the soup kitchen, and we were running late. Grandmother told me to hurry it up and get dressed, and yes, I had to come, because they will need all the extra hands they can get. What the hell? I like saying hell.

So I pulled on my white baby doll dress and flip-flops and got in the Roadmaster, slamming the door extra hard to make a statement. It did not make a statement. The door weighs about two hundred pounds, so I barely got it to latch properly. When we got to the soup kitchen, there was a bunch of commotion, like everyone was super hungry and was wondering what the holdup was. Like, where are the people who are supposed to feed us? A bunch of them looked mad. It was *very scary, like I was in a real zombie movie. Attack of the Homeless Grownups! Only there were tons and tons of kids, too, because it's summer and school is out. Even the children looked mad. I thought homeless people would be all thankful and all glad to have someone to give them food. I am just a 7th grade girl. I stay summers at my grandmother's because my mom is an alcoholic. I hate being dragged to serve a bunch of people who treat me badly while I serve them squash, field peas, and cornbread with a sort of happy face. I think homeless people take advantage of nice people. But my grandmother said they are not all homeless and that many have genuine needs. And that it's not our job to determine who is taking advantage and who is in genuine need, like people with mental illnesses or the elderly who cannot work. And the kids. We do our job and trust the Lord to send the folks who need us most, she says. Well, today was the day we were offering ice cream sandwiches. That was it. It was hotter than hell outside, and everyone just wanted their ice cream. After the ice cream sandwiches were passed around, everyone calmed down. I will never take an ice cream sandwich for granted again. That was this morning. We've been back home long enough for me to watch the white guy with the fro do a painting on PBS. He talks all soft, like he knows old people are probably sleeping during his show, and he doesn't want to wake them. My grandmother likes to paint with him. I do not paint. I am bored to death. I will write down more of The Huey Incident. The last thing I want to do is write it down. Because very soon I'll have to tear this whole diary to shreds and eat it. To dispose of the evidence.*

It started on a day like this: Mrs. Hall had us dissecting in science. First, we cut up worms, then frogs, then rats. Not all on the same day or anything because that would be a little too Pet Cemetery for us 7th graders. It was always gross, but after doing it a few times, you become a pro. Plus, the "subjects" have already been drained of blood. I hated the rats the most because they have fur, and I have heard that rats are smarter than people. There was a special trashcan Mrs. Hall set up where we were supposed to place the rats after our lab, so that she could take them to the animal graveyard or something, but Bert Smith did something really bad. When Mrs. Hall turned her back to write on the board, he cut the head off his rat and chased some of the girls with it behind the lab tables. I thought I would get sick and felt very sorry for the rat, even though it was already dead. Mrs. Hall stopped talking and put down her chalk. She yelled, Cut it out! She couldn't see what it was everyone was screaming about. Bert got still, faked like he was going to throw it at me, but suddenly tossed it in the regular classroom wastepaper basket. But I imagined a rat's head hurtling towards me anyway, and I felt like I might lose my lunch of deviled ham and Cheetos. So I concentrated on the chalkboard, which had a picture of a rat kidney on it. It looked so much like a swimming pool that I imagined myself floating on a raft with a bright blue sky overhead, until the feeling went away. On a scale of things that are scary, a flying rat's head is equal to a wolf spider jumping into your mouth. And it gave me an idea: I immediately thought of Huey The Pudding Stealer. The bell rang, and my classmates packed up their book bags and pushed their way out of the biology lab. But I kept my eye on the wastepaper basket. I stepped out of the classroom and waited in the corridor for Mrs. Hall to walk to the teachers' lounge. I prayed under my breath that she would not glance at the wastebasket. When the coast was clear, I ripped 3 sheets of paper from a notebook and used them like a glove to get the thing out. No one would ever suspect a nice girl with blond hair to be in possession of a dead rat head. I have never written this before, so I am going to need to take a break from these details. I cannot believe that I, Mary Beth Green, a straight B student, did such a thing. And if anyone is to read this and tell anyone: I will wait until you fall asleep and superglue your left finger inside your right nostril....X

22

DETECTIVE METZ

Mary Beth

More banging comes from under the house. I could make a fortune giving haunted house tours. We could turn off all the lights and let people walk through while the plumbing is being installed. Not only would it be terrifying, but the money earned could subsidize the cost of the new pipes and maybe even the port-o-let. It has taken a lot longer than the one week to have the plumbing up and running. The plumbers tell me I'm not the only person in town to need a plumber.

The person who took our pipes managed to do it in a flash, virtually under our noses. I have a feeling whoever was responsible could install them much quicker than the Laurel and Hardy that Clean Flush sent over. The pipes must have been stolen some unusual day when the house was empty. And what became of all that copper? It doesn't seem like someone could walk into a pawnshop with a truckload of copper and hock it like a television to be displayed next to diamond rings and roller blades. I keep thinking how I brought all this on myself. It's what they call Karma. You sow, you reap. Pilfer a dog, lose your pipes.

It's about 7 a.m. on Saturday, and I'm sitting on the front porch drinking coffee. Mr. Littrel across the street is doing his wind-up man routine. Wearing the same outfit as always: blue, button-down shirt and khaki pants. He comes home from work and goes directly into the house without looking around to wave or acknowledge any of the neighbors, then an hour or so later he walks outside and does yard work in that same outfit. He lives in one of those traditional brick homes, painted white. He leans a ladder against the house to get up on the roof in the redundant outfit. I wish one time he'd look my way, create a little crack for me to squeeze into his life, so I could invite him over. The Beatles said it well when they sang that song about all the lonely people.

I'm about to stand up and go back in the house to help Mavis fix the Saturday breakfast when up drives a police car and parks out front. I hope they figured out who took the pipes. It's a little too late to put it all back under the house, but maybe I could sell it to the Treasury Department, so they could crank out some more pennies. Or to that Franklin Mint to make those worthless keepsake collectors coins.

"Hey there, Officer," I say as he walks up the sidewalk towards the porch. I'm still wearing my old pink bathrobe with the coffee stains, and I've got big-time bedhead.

"Hello," he says. "Detective Metz." He reaches out his hand for a shake.

"I hope you're not here to arrest me for indecent exposure," I say, standing up.

Detective Metz smiles this wide, white smile and tells me he's not the Fashion Police. He says, "I'm here to speak with Mary Beth Green."

"I'm her. Tell me you caught the plumbing pirate."

"I heard about that," he says.

Detective Metz has yellow hair and brown eyes. I'd surmise he's younger than me, say thirty. But who knows? He could be fifty. It's hard to tell with men sometimes. Lately, I've started guessing how old men are, then tack on an extra ten years for good measure. I guessed Terry Dorrie was thirty-five. So I suspect he's more like forty-five. You can tell Detective Metz is one of those pretty boys who is used to getting a lot of attention from women. Like he expects women instantly to be attracted to him, so even though I wish I wasn't wearing the pink robe, I assure you I have no desire to impress him.

"No, ma'am, this is not about pipes. I'm actually here for a more disturbing reason."

"A more disturbing reason?"

What could be more disturbing than a woman stealing a dog from the fenced yard of a stranger? Then dyeing it black. If I were someone who could faint really good, I would try it right now to distract Detective Metz. But I'm not. So I look at the ground, and say, "Okay, sock it to me."

He says, "Can you identify the subject in this photograph?" Detective Metz holds up a picture of what I expect to be a white poodle. When I look up I see the smiling face of a person I know well.

"That's Ned," I say.

"So, you know this man?

"Yes. He's not in trouble, is he?"

I start thinking maybe Ned got caught buying, selling, or consuming an illegal substance. I'm suddenly relieved he moved out of the carriage house. I start imagining the carriage house becoming a den of drug dealers, and other unhappy people. Drug dealers can attract violence. And I may have narrowly avoided a shoot-out in my backyard—a dead body in the lemon verbena, blood dripping from the daffodils—while Share Group is peacefully underway in the main house.

"Actually, Ms. Green, he's deceased."

"Deceased? But not like...dead?"

Detective Metz nods.

This can't be true. I look at the photograph again. It's really Ned. Cute, sweet Ned.

"When was the last time you saw him?" asks the detective.

I feel like I've had the wind knocked out of me. When I try to form words, my tongue acts as if my mouth is stuffed with sand; it doesn't want to cooperate.

"Well, I guess…it was last Wednesday…no…two Wednesdays ago? When he came to a meeting we have here."

"Do you remember if he was going anywhere later? Meeting anyone?"

I shake my head. "No. It's not something he would have told me."

"Tell me what you do know about Ned," says the officer.

Remembering Ned and his crazy dreams and him showing us the worm at Share Group makes me want to cry. I'm getting that prickly sensation in my nose, and it's creeping up to my eyes.

"Ned is one of the nicest people you'll ever meet. He rented from me for one year and came to the Share Group regularly. When he lived in my carriage house, he'd come over for breakfast sometimes, so we got to talk a little. I know for a fact he did a good business as a computer programmer and played a lot of video games. When our plumbing was stolen, he moved out and, like I said, he wasn't here for our last Share Group meeting."

I feel a knot rising in my throat, so I swallow hard to keep from completely losing it in front of Detective Metz.

"Yeah, we figured that out. The video game thing," says the detective. "But what is Share Group?"

I define Share Group for the officer and invite him to join us. I believe law enforcement could use some sharing time as much as anybody. The police deal with situations most people would find traumatizing on a day-to-day basis. Take the officer who found Ned, for instance. Even worse, think of the folks who investigate serial killers, like Jeffery Dahmer. How would you handle being on a regular patrol, doling out speeding tickets, reprimanding jaywalkers, pursuing bank robbers, to suddenly be called to a disturbance in a house? You go to that house and open the refrigerator, and there, staring you in the face, is a human head. I think of those officers. They could use some share time.

"Thanks for the invitation," he says. "Can I get a list of names of those present the last time you saw Mr. Hillman alive?"

I go down the list, naming everyone from Mavis to Marcelle, from Terry to Lonnie Jr. When I mention Manchild's name, the detective says, "Manchild Guccio comes to your meetings?"

"I don't know his last name, but I doubt there are many people named Manchild in the world. He rarely came. Do you know him?"

"He's scum. I wouldn't put anything past him."

"Are you serious? I wouldn't want to be left alone with Manchild anywhere, but I can't see him killing Ned. They barely knew each other."

"Have you seen him lately?" asks the detective.

"Come to think of it, the last time I saw Manchild was the last time I saw Ned." I'm starting to get a bad feeling. Detective Metz writes on his notepad and questions me for anything else I remember about Ned.

"He had vivid dreams," I say. "He was always telling us his dreams like they were something that really happened to him. It also seems like he may have...I don't want to say. Well, he's dead, so I'll say...I'm pretty sure he consumed a lot of marijuana and maybe other drugs. Not that I knew from spending private time with him or anything. He was only like, what? Twenty-three?"

"Thirty-four."

"Thirty-four?" Here's a good example where I should have tacked on the extra ten years.

"Tell me about the last time you saw him alive," says the officer.

"Wait," I say. "Why are you asking me all these questions? How did he die?"

"It's not apparent."

"When did you find him?" I ask.

"This morning. The landlord, the guy who owns the restaurant downstairs, Mr. Stavros, said he'd been noticing a bad smell for a few days but

114

couldn't tell if it was coming from his place of business or what."

I'm going to be sick.

"Know anything about this Stavros?"

"He's Greek. It's his restaurant. That's all I know," I say. "Why are you asking about him?"

"It's nothing. Just that it seems you and your friends may have been some of the last people to see him alive and then Mr. Stavros," says Detective Metz.

"I'm pretty sure that Share Group was the last time. You don't think it was gang-related do you?"

The officer looks surprised. Maybe he's surprised I put those things together in my head so fast.

He says, "Ma'am, there was nothing to indicate this man was involved in gang-related activity. Although he may not have been completely law-abiding in all areas of his life, few people are."

He goes on to say how everyone has some kind of skeleton in the closet. Then he says, "Even you, Ms. Green."

This comment makes me uncomfortable. Does he think I killed Ned? He couldn't possibly know about Floyd. Maybe he's implying I stole my own plumbing. Whatever it was, he asks me to come down to the station for more questioning.

When I return home from the police station I throw my purse over a chair. The TV is on in the living room, and a couple of people are drinking coffee. Somebody shouts, "Buy a vowel!" Then I hear a voice from the TV saying, "I'd like to buy a vowel, Pat."

Mavis is standing at the kitchen sink giving Floyd a bath. Her eyes are red and puffy. She took the news about Ned pretty hard. We all did. It's hard to believe. One day a person is very much alive, telling you his dreams, the next day he's packed up and gone from the world forever.

"How'd it go, darlin?" Mavis asks.

"Fine. They're gonna ask the whole group to come in at some point for questioning. I don't get that."

"What'd they say kilt him?" She sniffs. "I bet it was them Hot Pockets, like Doyle was sayin.'"

"People shouldn't suddenly die from eating a Hot Pocket, unless they choke on it. If he choked on his Hot Pocket or one of his frozen yams, it would be pretty clear."

Mavis drains Floyd's bath water, and Floyd shakes a bunch, getting wet dog all over the kitchen counters.

"I forgot about Doyle's prediction," I say. "It all seemed pretty silly at the time. What was it he said about Ned?" I can't believe I'm seriously inquiring about a Doyle Stubb grocery reading.

"Doyle'll remember. Ask him," says Mavis, fluffing up Floyd's fur like she's a celebrity stylist or something.

The strange thing about being questioned at the police station was the line of questioning. No one came right out and said Ned was murdered, but the implication was in the air. Not really in the air, but it was like the police were trying to get at something. The detective asked things like:

"Were you intimate with Nedbolyth Hillman?"

"Nedbolyth? No."

"Did you buy drugs of any kind from Mr. Hillman?"

"Of course not."

"Did Mr. Hillman ever behave in such a way as to alienate or anger certain people?"

"Ned? I can't imagine anyone being angry with him."

"Was Mr. Hillman late paying his rent when he lived in your boarding house?"

"Never."

"To your knowledge, did Mr. Hillman own a gun or any type of weapon?"

"I happen to be positive he owned a Nerf gun and a lightsaber."

"I'll take that as a no," he said, typing into the computer. "What about pets? Did Mr. Hillman own, to your recollection, any type of aggressive pet?"

"He once owned a hamster called Sid Vicious."

"I'm talking Rottweiler or venomous snake. Pets of that nature, Ms. Green."

I shake my head. "Any idea how he died?" I asked.

"That information is confidential and still under investigation. I advise you and your friends not to leave town," said Detective Metz.

"Leave town?" I said. "I guarantee we're all going to stop our lives here in Brightleaf until we know what happened to Ned."

23

SLEUTHING

Everyone is present and accounted for. The regulars at least: Vanessa, Winslow, Chauncey, Eleanor, Mavis, Jimmy and his under painters, Baby George and Phil. Terry and Doyle are here, too. I asked Doyle to please make a special appearance. As much as his lazy eye bothers me with its probing, inquisitive way, I've softened when it comes to him. I've gotten to know him enough to believe he wouldn't use his powers for selfish purposes.

Everyone picks a seat in the circle, and I say, "I know it's only Monday, so I appreciate ya'll coming out to discuss this Ned thing."

Winslow fiddles with an unlit cigarette and says in his deep, slow voice, "From what I know of Ned, he stuck to himself, but was not necessarily introverted. And I do not believe he was murdered."

"I don't either," I say.

"You don't?" asks Eleanor. "Then why do the police think that?"

"I'm not sure why the police think that."

"Maybe it was suicide!" says Jimmy. "Or accidental suicide. Like mistaking rat poison for sugar or something."

"I didn't know Ned well," says Terry, "but he'd have to be sleepwalking to mistake rat poison for sugar…isn't it blue?"

"Sleepwalking! Didn't Ned sleepwalk?" asks Eleanor. "That night he turned on the TV after he went to sleep? Remember? He told us about it."

"You think he was really sleepwalking?" I ask. "Maybe. What was his dream about anyway?"

Baby George leans back on the sofa and says, "The ghost of the Fonz turned on his TV." Baby George's clothes are splotched with dried paint from the neck of his shirt down to shoes.

Phil says, "That was *me*. I have a ghost in my truck."

"Phil, it's your liquor bottle that's haunted," says Winslow.

Jimmy says, "Baby George remembers right. Ned was having a dream the Fonz saved him from Evil Otto or something."

Mavis wrinkles her forehead, making it look like a topo map, and says, "What's a Evil Otto?"

Chauncey says, "Evil Otto is a video game villain. He's pretty scary."

"Sounds Nazi," says Terry.

"That's the funny thing about Evil Otto," says Chauncey. "He's terrifying, but he's just a smiley face."

"That's hardly scary," says Eleanor.

"I don't know," says Winslow. "Smiling villains are pretty disturbing."

"Exactly!" says Chauncey.

"I think the police should explore the sleepwalking a little more," says Winslow. "That should be in his file."

"It wouldn't hurt," says Terry.

I turn to Doyle, who's been quiet this whole time.

"Do you remember what you told Ned the night of the grocery reading?"

Floyd is fast asleep on his lap. Doyle absentmindedly strokes his fur. I take a close look at his hands. Doyle's fingers and nails are truly angelic, as Mavis said. What I wouldn't give to be in Floyd's place right now.

Doyle's good eye looks at me, but the lazy eye seems to be recollecting. He says, "I vividly remember the detailed grocery list of each person present that evening."

Apparently the lazy eye has a photographic memory.

That eye casually rolls towards Terry and lands, searching. Good thing Terry doesn't notice because he might get all hot under the collar and stomp out again.

It bothers me I don't know what Doyle saw in Terry's receipt. A tingling runs up my arm, and I start studying him, looking for whatever mysteries Doyle may have uncovered. Terry is leaning back in his chair, looking at the ceiling. He has a cup of coffee in one hand, and his other idly runs through his hair. He sure is handsome. And seems so nice. He looks at me and smiles. I hope to God that is not an Evil Otto smile because that smile could easily lure me down a dark alley.

Doyle returns his gaze to me and says, "I warned the young man about a certain video game obsession, but the presence of frozen spinach on his receipt indicated that he could, if desired, live a productive life."

"Why frozen spinach? I ask. "Why not canned?"

Doyle says, "The same. I explained that evening, yet not in depth. The presence of any form of spinach signifies a higher consciousness making decisions for the betterment of the individual, thus overriding the baser, more carnal desires created by a lower level body-mind agreement."

"Whatever," says Jimmy. "That is why I exclusively eat my own organic free-range boogers, instead of the steroid-infused boogers of body-builders. It's my higher consciousness leading me to imbibe such purity."

Jimmy, Baby George, and Phil fall all over one another laughing.

Baby George gasps for air, then says, "Yeah, we only put the finest USDA boogers in our burgers."

"Ya'll is stupid," says Vanessa.

I ignore them, as does Doyle, and say, "I guess he never ate it."

Eleanor says, "Ate what?"

Baby George and Phil bust up laughing again.

"I guess I'm wondering if Ned would still be alive if he'd eaten his spinach. Or maybe he did eat it and died anyway."

I've just about dozed off when Mavis knocks on my door.

"You 'sleep yet?" she shouts in a really loud whisper.

I'm quiet for a few seconds, making believe I'm out cold. Then I hear her say, "Sorry, Doc, looks like she's already asleep. Call in the mornin?"

"Mavis," I say in a groggy voice. "I'll take it."

Mavis tiptoes into my room and hands me the phone. I click on the lamp and murmur into the phone, "Is everything okay?"

"Hey, Mary Beth. I didn't think you'd be in bed yet. We can talk in the morning."

Terry has never called this late. It might be important. If I tell him to call back tomorrow, I doubt I could get back to sleep; I'd toss all night, wondering what he wanted. Wondering if he needed to inform me that he's one hundred percent sure that Floyd is Champagne. Or maybe he remembered something about Ned. Even more unlikely, and I shouldn't think about it...but I wonder if he really thinks I'm beautiful, like he told Marcelle in front of the whole group.

I say, "No, no, I'm awake. What's up?"

"I would have waited to call in the morning, but for some reason I felt like I should let you know sooner rather than later." He pauses.

Maybe Terry is moving away. If he's moving I'll wish I'd been nicer to him while he was here.

Deciding to take the concerned approach, I say, "Whatever you have to tell me, I'm here for you."

"I thought I should tell you that my ex-wife is moving back to Brightleaf."

"Your ex-wife?"

Come to think of it, I'd forgotten Terry was once married. It's hard for me to imagine Terry married. I try to picture the former Mrs. Terry Dorrie. The doctor's wife. Probably all glamorous and tan. Probably the owner of seventy-five pairs of shoes, hostess of fabulous galas, and fluent in French. The thought of her and the fact that *she* left him, makes me mad.

"Why would you need to tell me?" I ask, trying to sound upbeat and less tired than I really am.

"She's moving in with me."

This is the last thing I expected to hear. Even more unexpected is the effect his words have on my being; the world seems to stop.

"Oh," I say. "Are ya'll getting remarried or something?"

"There is no way in hell I'm remarrying my ex-wife." The New Jersey in him is totally coming out. "It's just that she recently returned from Germany and wants her dog. I told her the dog ran away, but she thinks if she's in town Champagne will come back. Champagne, that's the dog."

"Your ex-wife is coming to *live* with you because she can't find her dog?

"Yes."

"Does she have to live with you?" I ask. "I mean, why can't she rent a house?"

"Why not live with me?" he says. "We get along fine, and I've got plenty of space. Also, technically she still owns half the house. We have some unfinished legal business, even though it's been three years since we lived together."

"If you get along fine, why did ya'll get divorced in the first place?"

"I meant, it will be fine."

"She can stay at the Rapturous Rest, if she wants. We've got an extra room or two." Then I catch myself and realize if Terry's ex lays eyes on Floyd, she will instantly recognize her dog, blue or no.

"Mary Beth?" Terry hesitates. "This isn't about love…or anything."

"I didn't think this was about love," I say, my voice rising an octave higher than normal. I lower my voice and say as calmly as I can, "I'm going back to sleep now. Thanks for the heads up."

I lay in bed looking at the ceiling. What's not about love? I'm certainly not in love. I barely know the man.

24

THE PLOT THICKENS

I've just dropped off the toddlers. I mosey on over to the police station to check on any new developments. I ask for Detective Metz and flip through a worn copy of *Redbook* while I wait. The cover advertises an article called *Must-Have-Sex-Tools*. I turn to the page to find out what they are. I'm a grown-up. As I flip through the magazine, I change my mind about women being perverts. There must be such a thing. If I based my knowledge of women on *Redbook* alone, we're a big bunch of sexaholics.

"The downside to the vampire phenomenon is that men think biting is sexy," a voice behind me says.

I jump and drop the magazine.

"Vampire phenomenon?" I ask.

"Page 75. I read it a few days back on my break," says Detective Metz.

"I wasn't reading it. I was only flipping through out of boredom. I never read trash like that."

Detective Metz laughs and asks me what I do read.

"*People Magazine.* That's about it."

"Oh, so less trashy."

"Detective, I was just hoping to find out how things are going with Ned."

"Mr. Hillman's family has taken him back to Virginia for the funeral."

Ned's family. I hadn't really thought about Ned having a family before, which is pretty dumb of me. I wish I'd thought to meet them. To tell them their son was wonderful. I knew Ned to be an honest, kind, and dependable renter. I wonder if his family was aware of his break-dancing skills. I should write them a letter.

"So the autopsy must be complete," I say.

"We have no plans to dig him back up, so you can safely assume, yes. I'm not at liberty to discuss the autopsy; however, we've determined what we believe is the cause of death."

"Are you going to tell me why you've been questioning people? And why you're acting like Ned was murdered?"

"I never said Mr. Hillman was murdered. It was just that we found some fishy things at his apartment, and the coroner's office has given us some interesting information, as well. Not everything makes sense. The case is still open."

"Still open? What doesn't make sense?"

"Ms. Green. As pretty as you are, I'm not allowed to tell you those things."

It's good to know I'm working the pretty angle. I hold myself up a little straighter and square my shoulders. Then I say, "Detective, you've questioned everyone who lives in my house, including me, so I think I have a right to know if I'm living among murderers."

"I can't be one hundred percent positive you're not living among murderers."

"What?"

"I don't know the probability of a boarding house owner living with a murderer. Aside from that, I'll tell you this one thing: We found a substance in his apartment, and it tested positive in his blood."

"I don't find that surprising. He probably smoked anything not nailed down."

"I guess one could technically figure out a way to smoke anything," says Detective Metz. "But…"

"But? It's gang related, isn't it?"

Gangs are taking Small Town America by storm. I know it.

Detective Metz looks annoyed. "Listen, we're talking about your friend. You want to know how he died. I'm telling you what I'm not supposed to be telling you, so listen."

He quietly says, "He had yohimbe in his system."

"I have no idea what that is."

"Well, then look it up. But I will say that it has been connected with some dark situations, including voodoo ceremonies."

"Voodoo? Ned was dancing around campfires with bloody chicken heads? That doesn't sound much like him. But then again, like you said, everyone has a skeleton in the closet. A secret."

"Also, we found a diary-type book on the floor next to his bed. It's hard to tell which parts of it are actual experiences and which parts are made up. He had quite an active imagination. But I doubt we'll find any secrets in it."

"I think you found his dream journal, Detective."

I start getting energized because we were just talking about Ned's dreams in Share Group.

"Clark," he says.

"What?"

"Call me Clark."

"Clark. Like I said, Ned regularly told us his dreams. It was Winslow's idea that he journal them. It's really interesting you mentioned that because just last night, we – the Share Group – were talking about how Ned may have been a sleepwalker. I don't know. It seems like sleepwalking factors in with dreams."

"Interesting," says Detective Metz. "Others investigating the case are looking into the journal. Personally, I think it's a waste of time."

"But I'm asking if you think it's possible that he ingested something or more of something than usual, *while* sleepwalking. It's just that I thought you should know that sleepwalking could have figured in."

"I'll make a note of it, Ms. Green. Anything else?"

"That was the main thing I wanted to tell you," I say. "I was also wondering if there was any spinach in his freezer. Did you happen to notice what was in his freezer?"

The detective stands, and I stand with him. "What does spinach have to do with anything?" he asks.

I don't want to get into cryptic spinach meanings. Then I'd have to tell all about Doyle, and it would sound dumb. So I say, "Ned was big into thinking if he didn't eat spinach he would die. That's all."

"Strange," says the detective.

"I know. Anyway, I don't want to tie you up any more." I pick up my pocketbook.

"Ms. Green, you can tie me up any time." His smile unsettles me, and he extends his hand.

I don't want to touch it. So I nod and say, "Thanks," pretending he didn't just say that.

Detective Metz asks, "Are you going out with anyone?"

I look at him like he just spoke Elven. I wish Detective Metz would act like most policemen, with that comforting, practiced, robotic air. I want him to be by the book instead of *Call me Clark*. It's disappointing to see his professional veneer crumbling before my eyes. I hate that I know he reads *Redbook* on his lunch break. However, I'm pretty happy to have the information on Ned. Maybe next time I see the detective, I should borrow something from Marcelle's closet. Lord knows how much info I could squeeze from him then.

It's Wednesday night again. Share Group is over and people are trickling out. Mavis, Eleanor and I push the furniture back in place, click off lamps, and gather coffee cups. Terry is hanging around to help. I know his ex-wife Jeanine has already moved in, even though no one mentioned it.

I drove by his house the other morning and saw a bunch of signs stapled on trees that read, *Have You Seen Me? My name is Champagne. I'm a white poodle, 12' tall.* Then there's this picture of Floyd from when he was still white. I doubt Jeanine realizes she described Champagne as a twelve-foot poodle. I was tempted to knock on Terry's door and tell her but didn't want to look into her eyes, in case she's like Doyle and can read people by their hairdos or something. I imagine it would go: *Longer than shoulder-length on a person over thirty-five is a sign the person wearing the hairdo is trying to act younger than they truly are—deceptive. Blonde means you probably bleach your hair, which is also misleading.* I drove on.

I ask Terry how things are going with his ex-wife and all. He tells me about her putting up signs and how weird it is to have her living with him again.

"It's strange," says Terry, "to come home from work and find Jeanine cooking dinner."

"For both of ya'll?"

He nods and says, "She's a great cook."

"How great?"

"So great that I feel guilty. She goes to so much trouble. Cooking has always been one of her favorite pastimes."

Always been one of her favorite pastimes. It's sinking in that Terry shares a past with Jeanine. They know one another in ways no one else could. Terry knows her fears and what she cannot abide. He knows her weaknesses and things that will set her off. There are passages in their lives that no one knows are there but them; they are locked doors to everyone else. To me. I shake myself out of this depressing revelation and say, "Oh really? Jeanine is that good of a cook? I'm impressed." More intimidated than impressed. I can't remember anyone ever saying much about my cooking. "What did she make?" I ask.

"This incredible lasagna."

Lasagna. Big deal. We eat that on Italian night at the Rapturous Rest every week.

He says, "Homemade pasta, layered with scallops, wild mushrooms and champagne sauce."

"Oh."

Terry smiles at the ceiling, like he's remembering every bite then turns a serious gaze on me. "You need to come over and eat with us sometime."

"Thanks. Tell her to make it for three next time."

"And the wine was out of this world. It was dry yet fruity, light yet loamy…perfect with the scallops and pasta."

He's talking with an expression on his face like he had the gastronomical experience of his lifetime and that he might just let himself die now. I do not know what to say. He's talking about his ex-wife's cooking, for Pete's sake.

"Wine, huh," I say. I rarely drink. Still, I'm jealous because it sounds like Terry and Jeanine are having a regular old home week, eating the meals and drinking the wine that doctors and their wives normally enjoy. Living the life they thought they'd live when they were first married. Next week they might host a fabulous gala.

I smile and nod. I love gourmet cuisine like the rest of them, but it's more sensible, budget-wise, to plan meals economically when cooking for a big crowd. I think of the only things Terry has ever eaten at my house: chicken tetrazzini, broccoli casseroles, spaghetti, Hungry Jacks, sweet tea. Beef Stroganoff. Nothing exotic. No wine. Terry must think I'm a regular Country Comes To Town.

"Glad things are going okay," I say.

"Yeah, me too."

129

25

THE HUSH-HUSH ALL WEEKEND THANG

"Where are you headin off to?" asks Mavis.

I've got my pocketbook and my keys in hand, and I'm almost out the door. "Toddlers, bank, Walgreens, library."

"You gonna check you out a book?"

"Maybe."

I plan to do a little research on the library computers, pull some books, and find some information on sleepwalking and this yohimbe stuff. I might as well look up information on video games while I'm at it. But I don't want to tell Mavis any of that. I'm pretty surprised to learn Ned might have been experimenting with drugs most people have never heard of. Then again, I didn't know him that well. For all I know, Winslow could be a Moroccan Shriner and wears one of those grand pooh-bah hats with the tassel on the weekends, and that would be none of my business. I've found over the years that people will not always tell you everything about themselves. I tend to tell it all, so it used to surprise me when I learned new things about people I knew fairly well. One used to be a Navy Seal, another previously married to a person other than the person to whom he is now married, and one looked and acted poverty-stricken but had millions. After a while, I figured that people like to keep to themselves, and it's none of my business. Kind of like Terry Dorrie and whatever he didn't want Doyle telling.

After spending about four hours at the library, including a couple of hours surfing websites, I've got about enough information on herbs that I could graduate from being a boarding house operator to a witch doctor. I probably know as much as Jimmy now. Not that I'll retain much of it. It was interesting to learn about all those helpful plants growing right in our own woods and even my own backyard that could remedy a headache, remove warts, and cure the common cold—free for the taking. I considered discussing yohimbe with Jimmy, but seeing as I was dealing with classified information, I decided to keep it on the down low.

I've got to say that the information I turned up leaves me shocked, and I'm worn out. But it's the kind of tired that comes from being really productive: squeezed of energy but happy. I'm starving and hope Mavis saved me something. Leftover chicken and dumplings would hit the spot. It's around 7 p.m. when I drive up behind the house, park, and walk through the back door. The house is quiet and dark except for the light over the kitchen sink and a blue TV glow emanating through the crack under the kitchen door. There's a bowl on the counter covered with foil. A note from Mavis says she's out for the night and for me to *eat up*. Thank you, Mavis. I pull back the foil, and steam rises from a homemade potpie. I hear Floyd whimpering and push open the kitchen door. I expect to see him standing by the front door, ready for his evening walk. Instead, Floyd is standing on his hind legs, paws on the windowsill, his nose pressed against the glass.

"What is it boy?" I walk over and peek out the window. I'm startled to see Mavis and Terry getting into Terry's car. Terry backs out of the driveway.

"Where in the world are they going dressed like that?" I ask Floyd.

Mavis

"Good Lord." I'm looking out the window and there's Dr. D coming up the walk wearin nothin but a long tan raincoat and some blue pantyhose. It ain't Doc's regular style. He done tried honkin for me, but when I didn't budge he came up to the door proper-like.

My mama had some child-rearin misconceptions, but she did teach me two important thangs: 1) Say thank you. 2) Do not walk outside if a man honks fer ya. Cleavon was the honkin type. My mama used to say, *We ain't runnin no curbside, drive-through service here. Let 'im bring his lazy ass on up to the stoop and knock fer ya.*

So here comes Dr. D, bless his heart. I run outside before he gets to the porch and yell, "Get your bu-utt back to the car before them neighbors sees you!"

I run out and hop in the car. Here I am, ridin in the front seat of Dr. D's Lexus, wearin my favorite bikini-bod t-shirt, blowin cigarette smoke out my nose, ready for some action and mystery. (It was hard, but I finally convinced my body to take up smokin again.) It'll take us about forty-five minutes to get to wherever. The whole way, me and Dr. D shoot the shit like always. Finally, I ask him where in the world we're goin. But Doc just laughs and tells me I'll see. So I says to him, "Well, I sure hope you won't be the only one there wearin them."

He says, "Not everyone will be wearing exactly the same get-up, but I promise you'll get an eyeful."

"Dr. D? Can I ask you a personal question?"

"Depends."

"Do you like ladies or men?"

"What?"

I take me a long drag on my cigarette, push the window button down, and blow the smoke out to the highway, and says, "I hate to tell you this, Dr. D, but them fairy pants you got on ain't attractive to most ladies. I maybe got me some men friends I could innerduce you to who would love 'em. And there might be a woman someplace, like France, who fancies her man in shiny tights, but not where I'm from."

Dr. D looks over at me like he's worried. But finally, we get to the secret place.

"We're late," says Dr. D. "I guess it'll be okay because this particular function will be going on all weekend."

"Sounds like my kinda party!" And I mean it. We jump outta the car and start high-tailin it over to the motel, the place where the hush-hush all weekend thang is at. Then...outta nowhere, I swear if I don't see somebody I ain't supposed to be seein.

"Dr. D, we're busted."

Mary Beth

Mavis and Terry are just getting out of Terry's car, and if I'm quick I can find a parking space and catch up to them. Mavis is wearing that god-awful t-shirt and Terry looks like a flasher. My heart sinks as early suspicions of his character come back to haunt me. This must be what Doyle saw in the groceries. I'm gonna throw-up. First Terry's ex-wife moves in with him, now he and Mavis apparently share some kind of sick bond. Or maybe they're on a date! I think of Mavis's note: *out for the night.* I must keep a professional air, as founder of Share Group and proprietor of the boarding house. But I must not appear to be holier than thou. I'm getting close now. Mavis spots me, and she jumps like a bee stung her. Terry has the same reaction.

"Mary Beth!" They both shout at the same time.

"Hey, ya'll," I say. "I couldn't help but follow you here. Ya'll looked like you were headed for a pretty interesting time and I didn't want to be left out. Where's Jeanine?"

Terry shakes his head. "Jeanine? Why would I bring her here?"

"Why, indeed?" My attitude quickly changes from smiling to interrogation. I feel like Doyle. Doyle would definitely say, *indeed*. So like Doyle I'm suddenly picking up on unspoken things. Things in the air. This tights and trench coat style is probably the whole reason Jeanine left Terry in the first place. Mavis says, "Mary Beth, you sneaky thang. You're supposed to be at the library! You know we'd have invited you if we wanted you comin, right Doc?"

"I can't sleep at the library. I had to come home sometime. And just in time to see you two driving off in those get-ups. Floyd alerted me. Even the dog knew something was up."

Terry says, "Oh he did, did he? Mary Beth, it's not that I didn't want you coming. It's that I didn't know if you'd appreciate this kind of thing as much as Mavis."

I say, "I'll have you know, you'd be surprised at the types of things I find entertaining."

"Is that right?" says Mavis. "And what type of thing do you think this is?"

"Honestly, I'm not exactly sure, but I can adapt. So why don't we all go into the hotel together?"

"Are you sure, Mary Beth?" says Terry. He almost looks like he could cry, the corners of his mouth bending down. Good.

I say, "Of course I'm sure. It'll be an adventure." But I feel a migraine coming on. The marquee in front of the hotel proudly exclaims, *WELCOME VOYEURS!* I keep walking. The sign doesn't bother Mavis at all; it gets her more excited.

Terry looks at me as if to say, *So does the sign give you a clue?* I pretend not to see the sign.

As we approach the hotel, I notice a couple ahead of us wearing similar gear as Terry: trench coats with tights underneath. I tell myself that I must be brave. I think I can be very brave until I realize the couple is Deacon Coons and Belinda from church rushing through the revolving doors. I stop dead in my tracks. These are the very last people I expected to see at such a vulgar affair. Looking back I try to remember times when the deacon and his wife may have caused me to wonder. Come to think of it, there was the time when Belinda was reading the scripture for the day, and the Bible slipped off the lectern. When she bent forward to pick it up she showed the whole church down the front of her blouse. The congregation thought it was an embarrassing accident, especially since she didn't notice. But now I wonder if she did it on purpose. And the deacon, he always seemed a little too friendly, didn't he? A little too huggy. And how about when Terry kissed Belinda on the cheek? At the time it seemed harmless... This is too much. My mind is exhausted from all these revelations. I don't I have the stomach for this any longer. I need to grab Mavis and go home, especially in case anyone sees me with this bunch and thinks I'm one of them. But Mavis is already inside.

The lobby has black marble floors and a high, mirrored ceiling, hanging with huge sparkling chandeliers. Mavis says, "I like this fancy motel."

Terry says, "Be right back. I'm going to check my coat."

Check his coat? Meaning, remove his coat from his body? I'm not sure if I should try to stop him or flee. We're so late everyone, including Deacon Coons and Belinda, is already inside the ballroom.

"Mavis," I say. "Let's get out of here."

Mavis puts a hand on my shoulder. She looks into my face and says real softly, "Now Mary Beth, this might be too much for you, baby, but I aim to see. I want to look and see what's happenin under that raincoat."

"But why?"

Mavis laughs.

I swear everyone is a pervert.

We follow Terry to the coat check, and as he unbuttons, I close my eyes and turn away. But Mavis, the voyeur that she is, is standing there with eyes glued to the raincoat.

Then there's the voice of a child saying, "Wow, are you Q?"

Q? What does that mean, Q?

"Nope, not Q," says Terry in a friendly way. "I'm Commander Dorrie of the U.S.S. Federation Starship *Wanderer*."

I open my eyes. There is Terry Dorrie, the man I've been reluctantly taking a shine to, standing there in a royal blue *Star Trek* body suit. Mavis is jumping up and down clapping her hands.

The boy says, "Cool. A real Federation Commander! Will you sign my shirt?"

"Sure, I'd love to sign it, but I'm a nobody, really. You should save room on your shirt for some of those celebrities in the ballroom. Some of those guys you'll recognize from the movies and TV shows."

The boy and his parents thank Terry.

Terry looks at me for the first time since removing his coat. He looks embarrassed like maybe he should head for the door. He actually does turn around like he's going back for his coat but stops.

"Well, this is me," he says. "Part of me, at least. I'm a Trekkie."

It takes a few seconds for me to digest this. Terry stands before me in a royal blue stretchy suit with a *Star Trek* insignia on his chest.

"Why the big secret?"

"I wanted to tell you, but I didn't want you to think I was a weirdo."

"I wouldn't think that. There are far worse things you could be doing."

"Honestly, I didn't want you to see me as some kind of character, like those other guys in your group."

"Some kind of character? They are just people."

"Ya'll work it out, but I'm gonna check thangs out in that ballroom," Mavis says. She adjusts her pocketbook, smoothes her hair, pulls up the waistband of her pantyhose and sashays off.

Terry gives Mavis a nod but picks up where he left off. "Just regular guys? Well, would you go out with any of them?" he asks.

"Well no," I say. "Those guys don't come on Wednesdays for a date. That's not what Share Group is all about."

136

Terry laughs and shakes his head. "So outside Share Group, would you get romantically involved with any of those men?"

"It wouldn't feel right."

"Are you attracted to any of them?"

"Of course not," I say.

"You don't find Jimmy sexy?"

"Jimmy? He's not sexy at all. He's always got on dirty clothes, has a scraggly beard, and I don't know...I just couldn't date a man who mixes his own medicine."

Terry bursts out laughing.

"But how about Jeanine? Sounds pretty cozy, what with her cooking teriyaki all the time and all that wine ya'll are drinking." I'm not going to tell Terry, but I drove by his house the other day, and his recycle bin was loaded with empty wine bottles. I imagine Terry arrives home from work carrying a load of chopped wood through the front door, while Jeanine, donning some cutsie apron, is busy cooking a gourmet meal. Then they lounge by the fire on a shag rug, feeding one another morsels of cheese, drinking themselves silly and reminiscing about the good ol' days.

Terry gives me a strange look.

"Jeanine drives me nuts."

"How so?"

"She graduates from sipping coffee in the morning to swilling merlot by noon. My neighbors tell me she spends the afternoon drunkenly yelling for the dog. By the time I get home from work, she's passed out in my bed, and my closet has been rearranged, my shoes are shined, and my boxers have been ironed."

"Really?" I'm fascinated and disturbed. "Did she always iron your boxers and shine your shoes? And is she still reinventing Julia Child in your kitchen?"

"Actually, this is all new. But she always cooked, and she still does. Even when she's drunk, she's a great cook."

"Just tell her not to do all that stuff."

"I've tried."

"What if the dog never comes home? Will she eventually go back to Germany?"

"She's positive Champagne will come home," he says. "I just have to put up with all the madness until then."

"By the way," I say, changing the subject. "Why does that sign in front of the hotel say, 'Welcome Voyeurs'?"

"The marquee?" Terry asks. "You mean the sign that says, 'Welcome Voyagers'?"

Oh.

How embarrassing. I was imagining a ballroom chock full of sweaty, half naked people teeming with V.D. I cannot express how grateful and relieved I am right now. Still, the fact I read it so wrong to begin with...I may never live this down.

"I guess you've got some friends in that ballroom?"

Terry nods and offers me his arm. "A bunch of voyeurs," he says, shaking his head.

We enter the grand ballroom. Deacon Coons and Belinda are both wearing *Star Trek* uniforms from the 1960s. Belinda looks surprised to see me, but they both give big waves. Terry waves back and says we missed Brent Spiner speak. He's the guy that played the character Data on *Star Trek: The Next Generation*—the robot with the white face. I admit to watching a few of those shows. I'm not totally ignorant about what's happening here. Terry points out Borg, Klingons, Romulans, and Cardassians but there are other alien people he doesn't recognize. He tells me he will find out because he's interested when they came into the picture. All these characters are wearing costumes that trick-or-treaters would envy: the makeup, the hairdo's, the complex tailoring. There is a whole family walking around dressed in *Enterprise* command uniforms, including an older boy, twin toddlers, and an infant. I point them out to Terry, and he says he thinks the mom and dad are taking it a little too far. I breathe a sigh of relief. I mean, the family is obviously having a fun time, and the little kids are getting a lot of attention, but I guess Terry's comment helps me to gauge his level of commitment to this stuff. Whether it's a diversion or an obsession.

What's amazing to me is all the *stuff* for sale. It's like a flea market on Mars.

Star Trek memorabilia of every kind is stacked on tables. The t-shirt table is making a killing selling shirts with sayings like, *You Will Be Assimilated, Daddy's Little Klingon*, and *Beam Me the Hell Outta Here, Scotty!* That last one fits my feelings perfectly right about now.

Other tables are filled with *Star Trek* action figures, bobble heads, trading cards, *Enterprise* replicas, and all sorts of hardware and knick-knacks one might find aboard a real starship, like phasers, tricorders, and bottles of blue Romulan ale. There is a Limited Edition PEZ dispenser set of Captain Kirk, Dr. Spock, Mr. Sulu and the gang for only $16.65 and tables loaded with *Star Trek* motion picture VHS and DVD sets. The books are interesting. There's the *Autobiography of Gene Roddenberry, The Star Trek Cookbook*, and, for those of us interested in learning Klingon as a second language, *The Klingon Dictionary*. Then there's *The Ferengi Rules of Acquisition*, for those of us interested in hostile takeovers in outer space. Several mannequins are sporting *Star Trek* command uniforms, some of which were worn on the shows and movies. The prices on the original uniforms way exceed the price of the replicas by thousands of dollars. This guy just won the silent auction for one of the original Jean-Luc Picard uniforms. I hear him say into his cell phone, "Honey! It's ours!" The Picard uniform is undoubtedly a new family asset. I can't stand my curiosity. When the man gets off the phone, I feel I must know some things.

"Excuse me," I say.

The man has a proud glow, like a new father.

"Congratulations on winning that auction," I say. "How long have you been collecting *Star Trek* memorabilia?"

"I'm not a regular collector, but my wife and I have been wanting to buy one of these for ages. I just can't believe we got such a good price!" They paid ten thousand.

I start wondering if Terry's uniform is real or not. We got separated in the crowd, what with me looking at all the stuff. I weave through the jungle of aliens.

"Hello, Commander! It's good to see you." I look over, and there is Terry being a commander, I guess. I walk over, giving his uniform the once-over. I doubt he paid ten thousand for it, but I have no way of deciphering whether it is the real thing or not. I stand next to Terry and face the man in a mustard and black uniform.

"Is this your wife?" asks the man.

"I wish," says Terry. "Bill, this is my friend, Mary Beth. It's her first conference."

"Nice to meet you, Mary Beth."

"Nan-noo, nan-noo," I say, cheerfully holding out my hand.

"What?" says Bill.

"You know, that's what Mork from Ork said."

"Oh, yeah. Good one! Well, see ya around, Commander."

"See ya, Bill."

"You wish?" I ask.

"Nan-noo, nan-noo?"

"Ya'll take this *Star Trek* stuff way too seriously," I say. "Anyway, how does one become a Commander? Do you pretend to drive a spaceship?"

I suddenly have this creepy vision of Terry doing all kinds of role-playing in his *Star Trek* commander suit. Pretending to drive a ship. Giving commands to those around him. Putting the ship into warp drive and lowering the shields, while those around him pretend to act on his commands. Thinking about Terry doing these fake things makes me feel weird, like my head weighs ten more pounds.

"No, it's more like an honorary title. I'm the president of our local chapter. Voted in."

"What do ya'll do at the meetings?"

"Talk about *Star Trek*."

"Seems like that could get a little boring. Seeing it's not real and all. The things that happened on the shows seem pretty limited," I say. "Not to put you down or anything."

"Not true," says Terry. "There are tons of scientific ideas and inspirational concepts *Star Trek* has introduced to the world. There's a lot to talk about. It's a fun way to socialize with a common interest, and we mix it up by getting involved in charitable causes. We visit children's hospitals and sometimes get asked to birthday parties. The costumes keep it wacky."

It all sounds fairly normal and even wimpy, in a good way. The *Star Trek* club isn't so different than Share Group. It's not a bad thing to be with a group that makes you feel all right for being nerdy.

"Have you seen Mavis anywhere?" I ask.

"I just saw her by the D.J. table."

The D.J. is playing oldies music on the other side of the ballroom.

"Why play oldies music at an outer space convention? I would think they'd play something more galactic, like *Star Wars* or something." We make our way through the jumble of people and excitement.

"We've got a Klingon who works at a local oldies station. He donates his time and music every year."

I check out the D.J. booth. Mavis is requesting a song.

"Can ya'll play, 'Squeeze Box'?" she asks

"'Squeeze Box,' by The Who. That's a fun song. Not very outer space oriented but neither is CCR," says the Klingon, who just finished playing "Proud Mary." "Give me a minute, and I'll get it going."

"I'd appreciate that," says Mavis. "That's my personal theme song."

Lord, when the song starts, Mavis starts dancing alone. She dances like she's in some kind of cowboy bar, stomping her feet with her elbows bent and fists curled into balls near her chest, and she's kind of galloping in a circle. She's also smiling big, and her eyes crinkle all over. Her hair is all teased up big and newly highlighted, and she's wearing a boatload of instant tanning cream. Mavis is very tan in a way only an old carrot can be. But she sure is charming, motioning to random *Star Trek* gentlemen to join her. She's now attracted the attentions of a Borg. Mavis is there, in the middle of the Trekkie convention, wearing her bikini-bod t-shirt, dancing with a Borg, to the words *Mama's got a squeeze box, Daddy never sleeps at night*. Mavis certainly is not out of place; in fact, she fits right in and is having the time of her life. She motions to Terry and me to join her. I don't budge and shake my head, but Terry grabs my arm anyway and drags me out to the dance floor with Mavis and her Borg. He's got more spunk than I thought. I stiffly give in to the music and notice that Terry is actually a pretty decent dancer—I mean, as far as dancing on a dance floor to The Who at a Trekkie convention is concerned. He doesn't act robotic, the way some men do when music starts playing and they're required to dance. He's having a good effect on me, and I begin to loosen up. Or maybe it's the music or the whole atmosphere. My migraine is completely gone.

Mavis

Dr. D brought a new t-shirt over to the house today, and you'd better believe I'm wearin it. It's purple and says, *Trailer Trekkie*. But that ain't nothin; Dr. D brought Mary Beth her own red stretchy *Star Trek* outfit. She won't try it on, though.

2⑥

DO NOT READ

July 21, 1990

Dear Diary,

Grandmother has her bridge club over and I have ZERO to do. I put on that record I got at the flea market, the Osmonds' Crazy Horses, and it could have been funny if I had a friend to laugh at it with me, the way Margaret and I did with the Perry Como Christmas Special last year. But now I would never laugh at Perry Como since becoming his devoted fan. I am serious. I would completely die before I'd tell a soul. That's what being bored does to people. Turns MTV watchers into diehard Perry Como groupies. Also being bored makes people who have nothing else to do write to a diary. So now I will finish writing my confession, otherwise known as The Huey Incident. Where was I? I have to go back and check. OK. I had the thing (rat head) in my backpack. I did not want to carry the thing in my backpack overnight. So I had to act fast. After school, I borrowed some tape from the librarian and took it to the girls' bathroom. I used the handicap stall, so I'd have as much space as I needed and would not accidentally drop the thing in the toilet, and taped the notebook paper around it, like wrapping a present. The thing suddenly turned into a gift. Then I pulled from my purse the tube of tan frosted lipstick, rubbed it all over my mouth...and I did it: I kissed the notebook paper with the gift inside. Then I scrubbed my mouth really good with toilet paper and washed my lips with actual soap. Red lipstick would have been an improvement, but nobody wears red except hookers. Then while I was running towards Huey's locker, I thought it might be a good idea to give the gift a name, like Otis or Curtis or Tony. I decided Tony was good. Not everybody locks their lockers because there is not a big problem with stealing at my school. Some kids put their locks on and make them look locked because they are too lazy to do the combination every time. I checked Huey's. It was locked. My head was starting to hurt, and I started to imagine that Tony was gnawing a hole through my backpack or threatening to rot on the spot. And then OUT OF THE BLUE Huey and two of his dorky friends, his fellow Indiana Jones fanatics, walk up to his locker and Huey opens it. I wish I had a periscope like in the movies so I could sneakily read his combination from around the corner. Then one of the dorky friends steals Huey's Indy hat off his head. The friends started running around, throwing the hat back and forth, keeping it out of Huey's reach like boys do. So I very quickly walked past Huey's locker and chucked Tony in there, praying to God he would see it, instead of overlooking it for several days. I walked away as fast as I could. I'm going to need to take another break in telling this story. I'll come back to it in a few days or months.....X

27

DOYLE REVEALS ANOTHER MYSTERY

Mary Beth

"It looks like ya'll two done kissed and made up," says Mavis to Terry and Doyle. "If I didn't know no better, I'd say ya'll was a hot item."

"I'm still holding out for you, Mavis," says Terry. He is wearing a pale blue starched shirt with jeans. The starch was probably fresh at 7 a.m., but now at 7 p.m., it's got a series of horizontal creases along the midsection.

Doyle says, "I would say the good doctor and myself have come to an understanding as to why I hesitated at his grocery reading a few weeks ago. I felt that I might be handling privileged information, so to speak."

The *Star Trek* thing was Terry's big secret.

Everyone is sitting around holding paper plates sagging with casseroles, Hungry Jacks and salad. We're all stuffing ourselves senseless before Share Group. Jimmy and Winslow are sitting side-by-side debating politics (Winslow is a liberal democrat, and Jimmy is libertarian), while Mavis and Vanessa chat about Vanessa's cousin, who is an actress in one of those prescription drug ads. Vanessa says, "You know the commercial with the smiling black lady riding her bike through a field of pink flowers, while that voice in the background tells you about all the terrible side effects? That your liver could die and you could get hives, and gout and all your teeth fall out? That's her." Eleanor is whirring about, collecting dirty paper plates, continually tidying, and wiping up stray drips and crumbs. She's my favorite boarder at times like this.

Terry and Doyle go back for second helpings. They stand near a folding table loaded with casseroles. "I still don't get it, Doyle," says Terry. "What kind of groceries did you see on my receipt that would tell you I'm a *Star Trek* commander?"

"I was alerted by the peculiar combination of pita bread, hot wasabi, and Fierce Grape Gatorade."

"You gotta tell me how you do that, Doyle. Nobody could guess that."

"The gift of grocery reading is inherent to the Stubb family."

"Inherited?" asks Terry.

"Inherent," says Doyle as he lifts a spoonful of broccoli casserole to his tiny lips. He pauses before saying, "Built into our genetic make-up."

I'd like to ask Doyle if he also comes from a long line of lazy eyes, but I'm trying to stay as quiet as possible. Listening and stirring the casseroles, pretending I've got something better to do than eavesdrop, and hoping no one will interrupt before Doyle reveals Stubb Family Mysteries.

"Wow," says Terry. He and Doyle both reach for the last biscuit, but Terry pulls his hand back and gestures to Doyle to take it. A little bit of déjà vu plays in my head. Like I've seen this before, only backwards. There goes one of my things against people from New Jersey down the toilet.

Doyle looks around while he takes a solemn bite of his Hungry Jack. His good eye looks thoughtful, while the lazy eye seems to scan the room vigilantly. He finishes chewing and speaks:

"Wasabi is Japanese; the pita, Mediterranean; and the purple Gatorade somewhat galactic. Combine foreign plus foreign plus somewhat galactic and you've got *Star Trek*. If per chance the purple Gatorade had been a strawberry Yoo-hoo, I would have said *Star Wars*. Although I've made no mention of the barbeque pork rinds and vast amounts of chipped beef on your receipt, I've learned quite a bit about you, Dr. Dorrie."

For a few seconds Terry appears concerned about the implications of pork rinds and *vast amounts of chipped beef*, but he changes the subject.

"What about animals?" asks Terry, motioning to Floyd. "I guess there'd be no way you could read a domestic animal, seeing it only eats what its owners feed it."

"Animals have a preference," says Doyle. "The dog makes choices concerning the dropped fragments he eats."

Doyle drops a piece of broccoli on the floor in front of Floyd. The poodle sniffs it and looks up at Doyle like he's waiting for some real meat. Next, Doyle drops a piece of lettuce. Floyd eats it.

"I've seen it all," says Terry picking up the broccoli with his napkin. "Whattaya make of that?"

Doyle says, "This tells us two things."

I'm all ears now, stirring the broccoli casserole till it falls apart and begins to resemble greenish orange soup.

"This dog has suffered exceedingly from indigestion sometime in his life, and wishes not to repeat the incident, explaining the overlooked broccoli. But...the choice of lettuce reveals something more diabolical." He pauses. "This poodle has been stolen from its original owners."

Doyle's lazy eye lands right on me. I'm not in the mood for challenging the lazy eye, so I look away.

"Stolen?" says Terry. "How about lost?"

"Stolen," says Doyle with his good eye looking real serious, like he's the Hercule Poirot of the canine community. Doyle is annoying now, like he thinks he's got a mystery to solve. Like he's been waiting to solve this his whole life. That lazy eye sure is a tattletale. It's screaming to be covered by a black patch.

Terry looks at Floyd and at me. I keep on stirring the broccoli. What am I going to do? I can't have Terry Dorrie finding out I stole Floyd from his backyard during an attack of neurosis. Even though it happened before he became my gynecologist and friend and whatever else he may be.

Someone asks about Marcelle, which thankfully shifts Terry's attention. At least he quits focusing on Floyd's gastronomical fortune.

It's around 10 p.m. I've just come in from the port-o-let, and I'm fixing to climb in the bed when the doorbell rings. Whoever it is, we don't want any. Mavis is probably in bed, so I step into my slippers, tie my robe, head down the steps, and look out the peephole. Terry Dorrie is standing out there holding a pillow under one arm and a bottle of wine in the other. I smooth back my hair, rearrange my robe, and creak open the door.

"Got any rooms? I'll pay my rent on time and clean up after myself," Terry says.

He's wearing the same wrinkly shirt from earlier, but his face has a weariness it didn't have at Share Group. Even though he's noticeably tired, I love how close he's standing to me, so close I can smell the soap on his skin. My heart beats a little faster as I let him in. I never in a million years would imagine Terry would want to stay at the Rapturous Rest.

"I can't go home until she's gone."

"Who?" I say.

"Lizzie Borden."

"I thought you liked her staying there."

"She's crazy. Also, she's made some…how do I say…"

"Made more lasagna?"

"No, more like…she keeps making romantic overtures."

"Really? What does she do?" I'm disturbed but also curious. I don't know how to ask without sounding eager to hear what Jeanine is doing. I try to imagine the kinds of things that would constitute an overture. Maybe she prances around in see-through negligees and lights candles all over the house at night. Maybe she asks Terry to bring her towels when she's in the bathtub or begs him to give her a back rub. I can't say I've ever tried to make any advances on a man, so I wouldn't know where to start. Jeanine must read *Redbook*.

He puts a finger to his lips and motions me to join him in the kitchen. He whispers, "I don't wanna wake anybody." He finds a corkscrew in a drawer, opens his wine and pours a glass. "Want some?" I shake my head, wanting to pick up the conversation where we left off.

"Are you going to tell me what happened?" I say. "Not that you have to, but I guess I'm just surprised to hear about the romantic overtures and all."

He laughs and says, "Lets see…for one, tonight I was stretched out on the sofa reading, and she came over and started massaging my feet."

"She did?" I practically gasp. I'm shocked that Jeanine would have the gall to massage Terry's feet. His ex-wife! What if Terry had a girlfriend? Doesn't she think about anyone but herself? I can just see it: Jeanine, blonde and svelte, acting all innocent about trying to find a dog, but all along she's waiting to pounce. As much as I hate this picture, there's something in me that can't wait to find out what happened next. I try to sound casual when I ask, "What did you do? You know, when she started rubbing your feet?"

"It was embarrassing, so I pulled my feet in and told her they probably stink."

"That's good." I hesitate, so I don't sound overeager then ask, "What did she do?"

"She told me she would wash them for me."

"Your feet? Wash your feet? You're kidding." I don't know how to ask this without offending him so just ask anyway, "So is that one of ya'll's things? From before, when you were still married? Foot washing?"

"Of course not," he says. "But I think she must be feeling a little love-lorn, and her living in the house again is making her feel like we're still married or something. I don't know."

Duh. Even *I* know that when you start having romantic dinners and conversations by the hearth in front of a roaring fire that it might-could make the individuals involved start feeling sappy.

"Lovelorn, huh," I say. The drama is killing me. "Anyway, what did you say when she said she'd wash your feet?"

Terry looks at me over his glasses and smiles. "You're pretty interested in this, aren't you?"

I look at the ground, like I could care less, and say, "It's not like I need to know or anything."

"Well, I felt sorry for her. So I let her."

My mouth falls open. "You did? What did she do? Run get a bucket of water?"

Terry shakes his head.

"So she didn't wash your feet?"

"She did."

"With a washcloth?"

"No."

"What? With some baby wipes or something?"

"Her mouth."

"I don't get it," I say.

"She used her mouth."

Words fail me. I wasn't expecting that. Then I say, "She cleaned your smelly feet with her MOUTH?"

Then he says, "She cleaned out my toe-jam with her tongue."

I'm speechless.

He looks really happy.

I stand up, "No way! I am sorry I asked. That is totally disgusting!" The image of Jeanine, that tramp, slobbering all over Terry's feet like a dog makes me ill. And to think he liked it.

Terry starts laughing.

"Hey, your feet belong to you," I say. "You are entitled to get your feet squeaky clean in whatever manner suits you. I don't care."

He is still laughing and shaking his head. "No, no, no. That didn't happen."

I don't know what to believe.

He says, "When she asked if she could rub my feet, I was blunt. I told her that I didn't think it was appropriate since we're divorced, and especially since she was the one who left me in the first place.

"I probably hurt her feelings, but too bad. Then she went to her room and put on a nightgown and came back out. She said she was setting the timer on the coffee maker for the morning, but I gotta say her nightgown would make a Victoria's Secret model want to hide behind a tree."

"Because it was so ugly?" I ask.

"It was a beautiful nightgown, and extremely sheer."

I was right about Jeanine prancing about in see-through negligees.

"What did you do?"

"I asked her what she thought she was doing and she said, 'Putting on the coffee.' That's when I grabbed my pillow and keys and left. I was scared to sleep in the same house with her."

"You think she's...unstable," I say.

He shrugs, "Who knows."

"Maybe she came back for you and not her dog."

I'm standing in the kitchen with my arms crossed over my robe while he sips his wine and sits on the counter.

I say, "I'd think you would be excited that she's making passes at you. Seems to me like a lot of men would like that."

He looks at me like I'm really stupid and says, "What kind of a person do you think I am?"

"I'm sorry. I don't know why I said that."

Then he says, "The Devil can sometimes do a very gentlemanly thing."

"What?"

"Robert Louis Stevenson."

"But what do you mean when you say 'the Devil'?"

"Come on, Mary Beth. I mean, it's not like I'm without defects, but I have standards."

"Maybe you should introduce Jeanine to Winslow."

Terry tilts his head like *that's not a bad idea*, then says, "Hey, you better get some sleep. Sorry to bother you with all the sad and torrid details of my life."

He's not bothering me one bit. I could listen to him speak with his New Jersey accent all night.

I show him the room that will be his new home until Jeanine leaves. Until the dog returns.

When I wake up at six, I'm keenly aware that Terry is somewhere in my house. I quickly get dressed, grab my toothbrush, face scrub and a washcloth, and head for the kitchen. Eleanor is already at the sink, brushing her teeth, so I start the coffee while I wait for her to finish.

I say, "You're up mighty early, Eleanor. Have some big plans today?"

Eleanor whacks her toothbrush on the side of the sink and drops it in a plastic baggie. "I have no plans. I didn't sleep a wink all night, thinking about Ned… We were kind of an item, you know."

I set the can of Maxwell House on the counter, flip the switch on the coffee maker, and say, "No Eleanor, I did not know you and Ned were an item. I don't remember you two being that close."

"There were things you didn't see."

"While he was living in the carriage house?" I ask. "It's a good thing I didn't know about that, or ya'll would have been out on the street *on the double*." Eleanor knows I wouldn't have the heart to kick her out, but I have to keep up the act. Sounds more like a fantasy, but you never know. Stranger things have happened besides Ned and Eleanor being a secret item.

"Good morning, ladies!" Terry enters the kitchen wearing a coat and tie with his laptop under one arm. "The coffee smells delightful."

"Dr. Dorrie?" says Eleanor. "What are you doing here?"

"I haven't had a chance to tell anyone you're staying here," I say. "If

152

you hang out a little longer Mavis is gonna heat up an egg casserole."

Terry pours himself a cup of coffee and seems joyous as a puppy. He tells Eleanor, "I'm here because I have company at my house, and there isn't enough room for me."

"Oh."

Then to me he says, "I'm gonna hafta miss out on that egg casserole. Early meeting, but give Mavis my best. He winks at us then goes upstairs for something.

"You should bring your company to Share Group," Eleanor calls after him.

"I doubt he'll bring his company," I say, pulling a coffee cup from the cabinet. "It's his ex-wife."

"Why is his ex-wife staying at his house?"

"It's a long story," I say. "Hopefully it'll be temporary." I wonder how long Jeanine will stay at Terry's looking for the dog. Surely she's got to return to her parties and yachtsmen or whatever soon. Not that I mind Terry staying here.

"Ned and I talked about marriage," says Eleanor.

Terry walks back into the kitchen and grabs his coffee cup. He heard it, too.

I'd like to call her on that so bad, but maybe she did talk about it, and maybe Ned nodded, stoned out of his gourd. Terry lifts an eyebrow, then motions for me to follow him to the front door.

"Is she serious about Ned?" Terry asks in a whisper.

"Can't tell," I say. "I have a policy against romances between boarders. Once they figure out they're in love they need to find someplace else to live, because eventually there *will* be drama. So I know for sure, or at least think I know, that when Ned was living in the carriage house nothing was happening between those two."

Terry shakes his head and walks out the door.

28

DRY CLEANING

Mavis

"Mavis speakin." I got the phone in one hand and Floyd in the other.

"Hey, Mavis, it's Terry. You doing alright?"

"Never better, Dr. D. I hate it that you missed my famous egg casserole this mornin cuz it was deee-lish, and it ain't very often I cook somethin that didn't start out in the freezer."

"Sorry I missed it, too. Hopefully, next time. Listen, is Mary Beth around?"

"MB just left to take the toddlers to the preschool, then she's off to who knows where. You want me to have her call you?"

"Actually, I was calling to see if she would pick up my dry cleaning. The laundry service delivered it to my house about thirty minutes ago, and it's hanging on the front door. I would get it myself but I don't want to see Jeanine."

"Well, hey, Doc, I'm fixin to head down to the Goodwill. On my way back I can catch a bus and swing by your place. It ain't too much trouble."

"Mavis, I can't have you do that. I'll just take my chances at lunch and pick it up myself."

"I already told you it ain't no trouble. You go on and save your energy for your ladies in the waitin room. I'm gonna fetch your dry cleanin like I told you."

"If you're sure, then thank you. You're a sweetheart."

"No sweat, baby."

The Goodwill puts out all the newest donations on Mondays. I like to get there real early, just as it gets laid out. It would shock you to see all the thangs people just up and give away. Like perfectly good stuffed animals. How I love me some stuffed animals. Lord a mercy. And the household stuff ain't bad neither. Once I got me a lamp that turns on when you touch it, turns off when you touch it. Who in their right mind would give *that* to the Goodwill for nothin? I brought that lamp home, and it tickled me for near a month, touchin that thang on and off. They didn't have Goodwill in the town where I'm from. Back then there wasn't much in the mountains. No Family Dollars or nothin. We pretty much made do with whatever hand-me-downs were circulatin through the relatives or whatever the Lystra Springs Baptist Church was handin out from the clothes closet. Most of the clothes that was passed along was homemade to fit a particular person and not me. The Goodwill is a one-stop shop. If your house burnt down today, you could go to the Goodwill and get you all the furniture, clothes, towels, bed sheets, and kitchen stuff you need for a hell of a lot cheaper than what you'd pay at the Family Dollar. And the Goodwill has the best t-shirts in town, but I ain't gettin none today. I'll have my hands full with Dr. D's dry cleanin...and this stuffed bear.

"Montague and Oak!" shouts out the bus driver, but I already know it's my stop. I take the bus cuz I never did get me a driver license, but that ain't never stopped me from gettin around. I've got friends who carry me when I can't get a bus, and my feet do the rest. I hug my new bear and step off the bus. I only need to walk two blocks and turn right to get to Doc's house.

Somebody sure is troubled about their dog bein lost because there's pictures of this white dog nailed to every telephone pole on the street. When I get up to Doc's yard, it looks like somebody done took all the leftover signs, and dumped them here—right in the middle of his yard. Every tree has a picture of the dog, and there are them little realtor signs that normally says, For Sale, except the dog is on near five of them.

Doc's dry cleanin is hooked on the front door. I lift the hangin pile of shirts covered in that silky plastic, and underneath is a big ol' poster of the same damn dog. Doc's ex is serious about finding it. I take me a good hard look at the picture cuz who knows? Maybe I seen it.

But it don't take me long to recognize this dog. I recognize it all right, like I would *my own son*.

I'm fixin to grab that knocker and bang till the ex opens. But I stop myself. If her lost dog is *my* Floyd, it don't make sense that Dr. D has seen Floyd two thousand times and don't know him. So maybe they ain't the same dog. I look at that poster again—look deep in the eyes.

It sure as hell *is* Floyd.

I says to myself, I says, *Mavis, you gotta think here. This here is a mystery. Dr. D couldn't never be the abusive pervert Mary Beth was tellin you about.*

So I set myself down at the bus stop and start to thinkin about how Floyd came to us in the first place. It dawns on me that one thang is for sure, that me and Miss Mary Beth Green is gonna have us a talk.

29

YOHIMBE

Mary Beth

Yohimbe is a dark herb. *A lust potion.* It is indeed used during occult ceremonies like Detective Metz was saying, as *a love sacrament for pagan matrimony.* I got all that off the *Occult Accents* website, the Wicca's answer to *Southern Accents,* I guess. I didn't peruse it long to enough to find out if it lists favorite pagan home decor, or cutesy pagan holiday meal serving suggestions like, *Use your old skulls for serving guacamole on Halloween!* I went straight to the page dedicated to yohimbe, and now I'm sorry I ever did. According to *Occult Accents,* after some pagans get married, they have an orgy that can last up to fifteen days with the help of yohimbe. *Fifteen days.* Just reading that made me totally exhausted and thirsty for a gallon of bleach. Yohimbe is also used in all-night raves as a hallucinogen. But taking too much can cause… death. Seems like too much of anything can cause death. I bet too much scallop lasagna could cause death.

On the bright side, yohimbe is the only other substance approved by the FDA to treat impotence other than Viagra. So basically, either you solve your impotence problems or *hello afterlife*.

There's a lot you wouldn't know about a person by just looking at him. Was Ned an all-night rave kind of guy? Who can tell? Everyone has a skeleton in his or her closet or, at the very least, undisclosed information they do not wish to share with the whole community. Now unfortunately, with my newly acquired knowledge, whenever I imagine Ned he's either tearing off his clothes under a full moon or in a graveyard stabbing baby dolls to death.

Terry is still renting a room here for fear of sleeping in the same house with his ex-wife. It's been nice having him around for the last week or so. He helps out more than the other boarders. Not that I expect my boarders to help out. I only require them to pay the rent on time and stick with the rules. But Terry takes out the trash, helps with the dishes, and changed a light bulb once. It's nice in other ways, too. We often sit around the kitchen table chatting with Mavis or dilly-dally on the front porch after supper.

I push open the kitchen door, and there's Mavis and Terry sitting side-by-side at the table, looking at Terry's laptop. He's explaining a parody news website, *The Onion*, to her, but Mavis does not seem amused.

She looks up at me and says, "Now that's a waste of time. There's already a bunch of crazy news to be had in the real world. Like that old lady who dug up her dead twin sister from the backyard because she got lonely. Baby, if I ever get lonely, the skeleton of Aunt Minnie ain't gonna cut it. And don' forget that full-grown man who pretended to be autistic to get ladies to change his diapers." Mavis lifts her eyebrows. She draws them on each day with eyebrow pencil, so when she lifts her eyebrows it's real dramatic.

I tell her I agree and open the fridge. "What's this?"

"Tuna Helper. Have you some. It's real good."

"Hmmm. What was for dessert?"

"Sarah Lee coffeecake. Saved you a piece." Mavis walks across the kitchen and pulls a piece of pecan coffeecake from the breadbox. "Had to hide it."

Terry stands up, pulls out a chair for me, and then pours a glass of wine.

"How'd your day go?" he asks.

"It was really good," I say, eyeing the wine. I pick a pecan off my plate and chew it. "Can I have some of that?"

"I hate to tell you, Mary Beth, but this isn't Cheerwine," says Terry.

"Oh, I thought it was. Please? Just a little in my coffee cup?"

Mavis says, "MB, baby, you're a grown woman. You don't gotta be hidin your liquor in a mug that way."

I say I'm doing it for other reasons. "I can't be having boarders walking into the kitchen seeing Terry and me drinking wine like we're on some kind of date."

"Why not?" asks Terry. "What if we are?"

Mavis looks at us, shaking her head, and says she's going to bed. She takes a quart of buttermilk from the fridge and pours some into a plastic cup with a Captain D's logo. She says, "I got me a bottle of Bailey's up in the room. Nothing better before bed than a glass of Bailey's and buttermilk." She whistles for Floyd, and they go back to her room, where he's got a dog bed in the corner.

I turn to Terry. "Boarder romance is against the rules. If my boarders think I'm breaking the rules, next thing you know everybody will start having boyfriends and girlfriends all up in their rooms and causing all kinds of disturbances and problems." Then I go into this long explanation of all the problems romances between boarders have caused me in the past, yelling and door-slamming being just the tip of the iceberg.

"So you're basically running a safe little boarding house. A place for priests and spinsters?" He smiles.

I tell him that there is nothing wrong with that and to quit making something good and regular come off sounding disturbing.

Terry laughs and says, "You said it, not me."

"It's not like I'm forcing people to repress their carnal desires," I say. "Nobody's making anyone live here. Let them go off and live in a motel or a frat house for all I care. I'm just one woman on my own. I don't have the ability to keep an eye on everyone. That rule saves me headaches."

"Sorry I teased you. But it seems so funny that you, the owner of the Rapturous Rest, cannot have a romantic evening. Even just sitting on a sofa watching TV with me scooched a little closer to you. It's harmless."

"I know. Hey," I say changing the subject. "I've got some news."

I hold out my coffee cup and wait for him to pour. He pulls a few bottles from the bag he brought home from the Wine Warehouse and asks if I'm a white or red person. I shrug. He picks a pinot noir.

I take a sip and must have made a face. Terry says, "You don't have to drink that, you know."

"I know, but I feel like I want to. To celebrate."

"What are we celebrating?"

"Everything I found at the library the other day. Before your Trekkie convention."

"It's worth celebrating?" says Terry. He holds up his glass for a toast, and I click my mug with his glass.

First of all, I tell Terry about the yohimbe and how Ned had it in his blood.

"Do they think that's what killed him?"

"They didn't know as of a few days ago, but Detective Metz could get in *big-time* trouble if anyone knew he told me. He acted like it was top secret."

"Detective Metz is feeding you top secret info, huh?" He raises an eyebrow. "That may not be all he's feeding you."

"Stop," I say. "The detective understands how much I care about Ned."

"How understanding of him." Terry gestures for me to carry on.

I tell him how I found out yohimbe is the bark of a tree that grows in

Africa. And how dangerous it can be if people consume too much. Then I tell him about the dark side. "You wouldn't believe what all I learned about pagan rituals and that type thing, even zombie lore."

"My god!" Terry clutches his heart like he's not taking me seriously. Then he says, "What are you saying? Ned was practicing voodoo or what?"

I shake my head. "I don't know. What I do know is *unspeakable* activities often revolve around that drug. Ned's dying was not right."

"Unspeakable?" Terry makes a face like he's not sure if I have my facts straight. Then he says, "I agree. Ned's death wasn't right."

"Also, the police found Ned's journal, the one where he wrote his dreams. Apparently they thought it was a hoot. Like Ned was a few clowns short of a circus. Loco. But I think there must be something important in it." I take a big gulp of wine. "I keep going back to Doyle and his prediction for Ned."

"As weird as Doyle is, he's actually got talent," says Terry. "He had me pegged."

"It's not a talent. Grocery reading is inherent to the Stubb family," I say.

We both laugh. Then we get into this conversation about the difference between talents and giftings, inherited versus learned. It's great, and I've managed to drink more wine than I planned.

Then I end up saying something that's been gnawing at me.

"How long to do think Jeanine will stay?"

Terry takes a deep breath. "Don't know."

"What if she never leaves?"

"She will."

"Do you think she hopes ya'll will get back together?"

He looks at me. "I hope she understands that's not happening. I'm here because she's driving me batshit. I mean, she opens my mail, calls my office four times a day, uses my razor, and sleeps in my shirts. She's totally invaded my privacy. I told you before she moved in this wasn't about love.

I'm just helping her."

"Be right back," I say.

I run down the hall to the bathroom, forgetting my pipes aren't fixed yet. I've got to say I'm pretty excited, though. He was talking about Jeanine when he said this *wasn't about love* back when he called me to let me know Jeanine was moving in. This emboldens me to act on an idea. I run upstairs, quickly change clothes, then, stumble a little coming back down the steps. When I get back to the kitchen, I hold out my coffee cup again. I think I'm starting to like wine. Terry is looking at something on his laptop. When he looks up at me, he laughs.

"You look really nice," he says. "Nicer than I imagined."

"You imagined me?"

"More than once," he says closing his laptop.

"Are you some kind of pervert?"

Terry stands and walks slowly over to me, smiling. I am wearing the *Star Trek* stretchy suit he bought me at the convention. He puts his hands on either side of my waist and says, "Thank you. You look beautiful."

"I don't look fat?"

"You don't look fat at all."

I hold up my face to his, closing my eyes, thinking this is probably about the time that he should kiss me. He's still holding my waist, and we're standing so close I can smell the starch on his shirt. The seconds tick past, and he still hasn't kissed me, so I open my eyes. Terry is standing there, staring at me in a way no person has ever looked at me in all my life. Like he's considering my very molecules. Like he wishes he could inhale me right here, on the spot. And then I'd disappear. All my particles would be absorbed into Terry. And as far as I'm concerned, he can do that. Make me disappear. So I close my eyes again, expecting something to happen.

"It's getting late," he says.

Then he takes my face in his hands. He leans in and kisses my forehead.

I open my eyes and look at him. I am so embarrassed I don't know what to say. Was it my breath?

"Time for bed," he says.

"Bed?"

"Good night." And he walks out of the kitchen.

I stand there in the stretchy suit, feeling all at once like a goddess, and a goddess rejected. But mostly drunk.

I down the wine in my cup and walk after him. "Hole it right there, buddy. You can't jus walk away fromme in my Cap'n Janeway outfit."

"Your rules," he says, shaking his head slowly. "Just following the rules concerning boarder romance. Sleep tight." Terry smiles and walks upstairs. I hear his door softly close.

I have a pressing reason to see Detective Metz, but I can't remember what it is. I just know I need to get down to the police station. For some reason, I'm wearing a very short skirt, and I keep thinking that my underwear is showing in the front, so I keep pulling my skirt down. When I see Detective Metz, he looks at my skirt, and then I realize I wore it to get information out of him. He approaches me, staring at my legs, and says, "Want to get some wine, Ms. Green?" I'm sick of him looking at me like that way, so I say, "You have many other fish in your sea, Clark. I have no plans to be another notch on your stick, another charm on your bracelet, another apple in your basket that you chew down to the core and spit out." Then Ned walks up. A certain light-headedness creeps into my being, accompanied by a blackness, and then I only hear voices.

Detective Metz says, "Nedbolyth Hillman, what are you doing here?"

Ned says, "Just taking a break from Evil Otto, man."

"How'd you get away?" Metz wants to know.

"Spinach, man. It'll save your life."

I open my eyes and see Ned. He's looking down at me lying on the pavement. I grab his hand.

Ned says, "It's okay, Mary Beth. I came to warn you that Otto is coming and that you better run."

Then Ned runs.

I'm confused until this smiling face comes bounding towards me. I freeze, terrified, and realize there's a good chance I'll be exterminated if I just lie here. So I make a subtle move to edge myself away from Evil Otto's smiling approach. My limbs are heavy, like sandbags. Otto yells, "Intruder alert! Intruder alert!" So I force myself to move. I am suddenly zipping through passages with electric walls. Somehow I know that if I touch the walls, I'll die. And now I'm running through Brightleaf; robots surround me blurting, "Get the humanoid." I easily knock them down and continue making headway for Main Street and home. I run up the front steps, so happy to be safely home. I reach for the knob, and Otto materializes through my front door. "Intruder alert!"

I'm doomed.

My head is pounding when I wake up. I'm not good at drinking wine, I discover. Also, I do not recommend sleeping in a *Star Trek* stretchy suit. After peeling off the suit and kicking it to the floor, I lay in bed for another fifteen minutes. Eventually, I slide one foot out of bed and then the other, pull on my robe, and open my bedroom door. Someone at some point slid a note under my door. It says: *Drink lots of water. Eat asparagus.*

I assume Terry put that there, and that he's speaking of my jumbo headache. We might have a can of asparagus in the kitchen. We definitely don't have any fresh. Anyway, I have other pain that needs attending that I doubt asparagus will make right. I hope to heck Terry won't be downstairs when I get there. The clock says it's ten, so there's an excellent chance he left for work an hour ago. I peek through the curtains. His car is gone, but the light is blinding. I put on my sunglasses and grab some Aleve from the medicine cabinet, a towel and toiletries, and tiptoe down the steps and out to the carriage house.

The carriage house was finished being newly plumbed yesterday afternoon. Just a few more days till the whole house will be complete with running water again. I haven't had a shower in my own house in weeks. We've all been taking our showers a block away at the Y. I turn on the water and wait for it to warm up. I start thinking how Ned was the last person to shower here. His skin cells are probably still haunting the drain. I get a chill just thinking about it, and I know I need to make something right, somehow.

Hot water streams over my face and rolls down my back like a hand of kindness spreading over me. I carefully massage shampoo into my scalp, thinking about Terry and Jeanine. For some reason, I equate my head pain specifically with Jeanine. Like if I'd never stolen Floyd, I wouldn't feel this way. I start thinking about what Jeanine must be doing now. She's probably waking up in Terry's bed, sleeping in one of his wrinkly button-downs. I imagine her walking to his bathroom, removing her clothes, and taking a shower in Terry's shower, washing her body with the same soap Terry uses. Now she's getting dressed, walking into Terry's kitchen, filling Terry's coffeepot with water, and cutting on Terry's TV, watching shows Terry would never watch. Jeanine unlocks the front door and looks out to see if anything touched the dog food on the front porch. Meanwhile, Terry is busy at work checking women's breasts for lumps, a chore which should make any man happy. But he is not happy. He's a stranger in his own home. His mail gets shuffled through, and his bed is slept in by a woman he doesn't love. He's needlessly suffered at the hands of Jeanine and become estranged from his own home because of me.

The coffee maker in the living room is huffing and puffing, so I stop to grab a cup, nodding at two people playing checkers and watching TV. A man with a thin, straggly beard and another man with meticulously combed hair and a shaved face. Both have the appearance of being a little over-exposed to the elements. This is the way I like it: people finding a place for themselves, but sometimes I wish I were less friendly. About now I could use a little privacy. This is my first hangover, and I don't want those homeless people knowing that I have this problem. They look up and smile and nod like they understand and welcome me to their world. All along I've thought of the people I reach out to as mostly crazy, and I'm the only one with the sound mind, able to offer a hand and some relief from this unforgiving planet. But now I see these people are not ignorant. They've seen people with hangovers their whole lives. I am them now. I am my mother.

I head to the kitchen and push open the swinging door. A steaming plate of poached eggs over blanched asparagus drizzled with hollandaise sits on the table. There is also a small glass of tomato juice on ice, with a wedge of lemon resting on the rim. A newspaper is spread out to the front headlines reading, "Death of Local Man Continues to Stump Investigators." A hot pink sticky note is affixed to the front of the paper: *Eat up. Talk later—Terry*

I sit down, grabbing the sides of the table, and ease my way into my seat. If my head didn't hurt so bad, I'd be amazed at this beautiful dish of food sitting before me. But being amazed takes too much energy. I take a sip of the juice and shiver as coldness flows down my throat. The eggs and asparagus taste like love, pure and simple. The eggs are soft in the middle, the way I like them. I can't say how they got here, but I feel comforted like an infant who's cried all night and now breathes steadily into a peaceful sleep. The eggs slowly absorb the throbbing in my head.

I study the photograph of Ned in the paper before me. He's all sprawled out on a blanket at some outdoor concert and smiling. He was sweet. I start remembering everything I learned at the library and my own dream. Last night I dreamt Ned tried to help me get away from Evil Otto. There was something about my dream. *Why couldn't you have listened to Doyle?* I ask the smiling picture.

"Detective Metz, speaking."

"Hey, Detective, it's Mary Beth Green," I say, holding the phone in one hand and my notebook in the other.

"It's Clark. How can I help you?"

"Um, Clark, I've been doing a little research, and I think I might be able to help in your investigation. I mean, I know I'm no detective, and it probably won't mean much to you, but I thought I'd tell you what all I've learned. Do you have some free time? When you're off-duty?" I figure if he's off-duty he'll be more willing to collaborate with me. I can tell him what I learned, and he can tell me what he knows without doing it in an official capacity.

"Are you asking me out, Ms. Green?"

I hate to have to deal with this man. I say, "It's only about Ned."

"Ms. Green, if you have information you can tell me now."

"I can't say what I want to say over the phone because it might sound far-fetched. I want you to take me seriously."

"Whatever. Yes, Ms. Green, we can meet for lunch. I'll have thirty minutes at one. I'll meet you at the Salad Station."

Even though I despise the Salad Station, I agree to meet him there. The Salad Station is a help-yourself buffet across the street from the police station. The lettuce is often wilted, and there is hardly anything appealing to put on it. It's not like it's a regular salad bar. The buffet is loaded with gelatins, tomato aspics, fake crab salad, tuna salad, chicken salad, egg salad, and fruit in heavy syrup. There's usually a congealed sheen over certain salads that I'm positive are teeming with E. coli. Brightleaf's idea of eating light.

30

HAZARDS OF BEING A
GOOD SAMARITAN

July 22, 1990

Dear Diary,

It has only been one day since I last wrote, but I need to finish *The Huey Incident* before I get too lazy about writing in a diary. I left off at the spot where I threw the rat head (alias Tony) into Huey's locker. I immediately ran towards the bike rack. Then I made a tragic mistake. I stopped and decided to circle back around. I shouldn't have wanted to watch him find it so bad, but I returned to the scene of the crime anyway and hid in the alcove where the bathrooms are. Those idiot Indiana Jones boys were still playing keep-away with Huey's hat, but it started to get old, and eventually they gave Huey his hat back. They talked for a few minutes, before the boys finally walked home. I was glad when those kids left Huey alone because I had to pee really bad but didn't want to miss the epic moment when Huey found his present. I watched him rummage around in his locker then...he got super still. I was so excited I wanted to laugh out loud because it was going to be so dang funny when he opened Tony. And that made it harder for me to hold in my pee. He stood up straight with the notebook paper package in his hands. He was looking at the lipstick print real hard. I watched him while he anticipated what could be inside. What was it that was sealed with a kiss? Probably he thinks his Young Indy act is attracting attention from some popular girl. I had to duck back into the alcove when he started slowly looking up. I thought I would die trying to suppress my laughter. I had tears rolling down my cheeks, and I had to get a hold of myself. I had to think of something super serious and unfunny, so I thought of Mr. Rogers, who is downright boring, even for little kids. I carefully peeked out again and narrowed my eyes as he slowly unfolded the paper. The Tony was in plain view. Huey was standing there wearing his Indiana Jones hat holding a rat head. Then Huey totally projectile vomited. And his head vaulted backward like a torpedo launched straight at the floor. Huey lay there on the ground, holding the Tony, covered in half-digested baloney sandwich from lunch. I hoped to God he was not dead. I have heard some people can die of fright. If I killed Huey, I would hate myself forever. I started praying super hard that someone would walk up and see him. Anybody. The janitor, a teacher, a cheerleader. But then I thought: What if someone finds him and sees him holding a rat head... that smells like formaldehyde? They will suspect it came from Mrs. Hall's lab. What if someone figured out a way to trace it back to me? If Huey was dead, I could go to jail forever. For murder. I needed to get the Tony back. So I decided I would look like I was trying to help Huey, in case anyone came along. When I got close to him, I said real loud for show, "Are you OKAY, Huey?" Then when I saw nobody was coming, I grabbed the nasty vomity rat head and threw it in the closest trashcan. Believe me when I say I was running on adrenaline and barely remember touching it. Huey moaned. Thank God he was alive! I wanted to hug him for not being dead. I told him I'd get help and planned to run down the hall yelling, HELP! But first I needed to wash my hands. So I stopped in the girls' restroom. When I stepped back into the hall, the mean old French teacher, Mrs. Bussy, was stomping out of her classroom towards me, all hunched and bunched (like a monster climbing from her cave). Her lipstick ran through the wrinkles in her lips, bleeding claret pink all around her mouth. We called her Old Anus Face behind her back. Somebody else made that up, not me. When I pointed to Huey, she looked at me with her watery eyes and demanded to know what I had done to him. My face felt hot. What had I done to him? Why couldn't I just be the girl who found him? A Good Samaritan? How about what he did to me? She looked at him like a poor little harelip boy, but she was clueless when it came to how strong he was. He was a tricky one. A pudding stealer. Mrs. Bussy called the paramedics, of all things. Next a stupid ambulance showed up with the sirens blaring. I tried to leave, but Old Anus Face grabbed my arm with her old wrinkledy hand and sharp fingernails and forced me stay, as I was "a witness" and "to get to the bottom of this." The paramedics talked to Huey and cleaned up all the throw-up. They handed him a glass of water, and someone called Huey's mom. When the paramedics finally went away, Huey looked straight at me and said, "What did you do with it?" "With what?" I asked. His face kind of contorted, and he screamed – and I mean he screamed – "You know what! Mrs. Frisbee's head! I saw you! You took it!" I wanted to die. I stuttered something about why would I want to take a head, and who is Mrs. Frisbee, and he goes, "My pet rat, of course!"

I lied. I lied in the principal's office; I lied more to Huey and Anus Face; I lied to my mother and told her Huey was delusional, that I would never in a million years touch a dead rat head, and she was so loaded that she laughed harder than I'd ever known her to laugh, almost choking on her

170

gin and tonic. That was the only time I was glad my mother was a drunk. And that, Dear Diary, was The Huey Incident. This is the official record, never to be seen by human eyes other than my own. And if anyone dares to read this and/or tell a soul, I will wait until you are snoring and put a wolf spider the size of a gerbil under your covers....X

31

THE SALAD STATION

Detective Metz sits across from me. Unlike in my dream, I am not wearing a skirt that rides above my crotch, nor a plunging neckline. I figure I'll tell him what I know, and if that's not good enough then I don't know. Maybe I'll tell another detective, or I'll get some kind of TV show to air my suspicions. I recognize that these days my opportunities for creating public awareness are practically endless. So if Detective Metz won't listen, somebody will.

"Aren't you going to eat, Ms. Green?" asks Detective Metz. He has a plate full of gloppy stuff. Egg and tuna salad running into orange Jell-O packed with gravity defying fruit cocktail.

I politely tell him that I'm not much for health food, that I'm more of a fried chicken and gravy girl. "Anyway," I say, changing the subject, "you think you got it figured out yet?"

Detective Metz unrolls his napkin and fork. He peppers his egg salad and sips his tea. He shovels a scoop of something in his mouth and while chewing says, "Nope."

"Well, I believe I can figure it out if you can help me with some things,"

"Hm," he says before eating a big bite of tuna salad. "Mighty bold of you to imagine you can figure out how a man died without even a fraction of the information the police have."

"It's not bold of me," I say. "You are a busy man, Detective Metz. How many cases do you have open? Seven? Seventeen? I don't know, but what I do know is that being a detective requires hours upon hours of work, interviewing people, and following up. Not to mention paperwork.

"Good grief, you might interview every single person living in five city blocks just to get a handle on one of these crimes." I let this sink in. "But not me. I only have one person I care about who is possibly involved in a crime. And he is dead. And he is the last person I would ever expect to be dead, so I am using all the spare time I have to look into what might have killed him. Are you able to do that for my friend, Detective Metz?"

He sits still, looking at me in a different way. He checks his cell phone and says, "What do you want from me?"

"I would like to take a look at Ned's dream journal."

"Ms. Green, it would be against the law for me to show you that journal."

"Why? You told me you laughed at it when you read it. If you think it's so insignificant, why can't I just take a quick peek at it?"

"I might let you take a peek at it if you let me take you out to dinner or something," he says.

"But we're eating together right now."

"Yep, and I've got to get back to work in ten minutes. Also, I don't have Mr. Hillman's journal on me at the moment."

I have no idea why I took Detective Metz up on his offer, except that I want to see that journal bad. I'm still frustrated with Terry after last night, too. The very first time in my life I've ever tried to do something sexy, I get turned down. Smacked down. The truth is, this is what I've feared my whole life. Putting myself out there and getting rejected. It's easier to protect your heart. A person protects her heart by not getting involved, by passing on opportunities that could turn out disastrous. I like pain-free living.

So last night I was like one of those jack-in-the-boxes you wind and wind, and it feels like forever until the top will pop open and the clown will jump out, but I finally did. I jumped right out in my stretchy suit, and it was like Terry was this big ol' hand that pushed me back in my box.

I wonder where Detective Metz and I will go tonight? I hope no place Terry will see us. But then again, that may not be so bad.

The doorbell rings, and Mavis answers it. "Well, well, well. What have we here? You're mighty dolled up to be lookin for killers, Detective."

"Hello, Mavis. Nice to see you," he says. "I'm not here on business. Is Mary Beth around?"

Mavis lifts her eyebrows. She looks at me while I grab my purse and says, "I ain't sayin a thang. But you know I want to."

"Don't be silly, Mavis. You can say anything you want."

"Does Dr. D—"

"Don't," I say. "Hey there, Detective. Clark. Ready?"

"Ready if you are," and he opens the door for me, and we walk out, leaving Mavis shaking her head.

Detective Clark Metz is dressed in casual clothes. This is the first time I've ever seen him without a uniform or a jacket and tie. Tonight he's wearing jeans with a black loose-fitting linen shirt. The top three buttons are undone, and it's untucked. He drives a black convertible Porsche.

"Pretty fancy car for a policeman," I say as he opens my door.

"I'm a single man. I don't need a Suburban."

"Have you ever been married, Clark?"

He smiles his gleaming movie star smile and says, "I've done my best to avoid marriage, but I imagine an heiress could persuade me." He laughs

174

at his own humor. "And what about you, Mary Beth? The eligible bach-elorette."

"Well, I'm not an heiress. So that pretty much eliminates me from the group of people who might persuade you to marry them."

"But you seem like the type of girl who longs for some kind of super-hero to come and swoop her up and save her from loneliness," he says, grinning. "You are lonely, aren't you?"

"Nope. That is not me. I have a house full of people who keep me company. Mavis and Eleanor and my other boarders. I seriously doubt I'll ever fall in love, but I might adopt a few kids. Some potty-trained ones."

"I hate kids."

"What? Who hates kids?"

"They're whiners. No matter how much stuff you give them. The older they get, the more ungrateful they get. Then you realize you've spent half your life and most of your money on selfish brats. I've seen it too many times. "

It's probably a good thing Clark has no plans to be anybody's daddy.

I ask him where we're going on our big date. There are a bunch of new movies I'm dying to see like, *Sixty Going On Seventeen*, *Around New York In Eight Days*, and *Coffee With Strangers*.

He tells me the theater is a bad place to take a date.

"Why?" I ask.

"For starters, each person stares straight ahead for two solid hours in the dark."

I start laughing. "It's not the same as staring at a brick wall. If the movie is brilliant or just plain awful, it's still fun to go to some all-night breakfast place to drink coffee and eat waffles until 2 a.m., talking about how amazed we were or laugh at how terrible it was."

"A Waffle Shop is not what I had in mind. And we already have a lot to talk about. Isn't that why you took me up on my offer? You want to learn more about your friend and see the journal. Right?"

"You have the journal?"

He pulls it out from under his car seat, waves it in my face and smiles. I make a swipe at it, but he shakes his head and says, "Patience."

I look over at Detective Metz driving along through the town, and I have to admit he is a fine looking man. He's got a handsome jaw and a good nose and chin, kind of like a young Robert Redford.

Finally, he turns into a neighborhood full of pretty homes that all look the same and says, "Welcome to my casa" as he pulls into a driveway.

"This is your house? I didn't know you were taking me to your house." Detective Metz's house is a new, one-story brick home. Just five years ago, this whole neighborhood was farmland.

"Thanks. I bought it a couple of years ago. I like having a lot of space to myself. Not as much space as you have in your fat manor on Main Street, but it's enough for me. Want to take a look? I might have a surprise for you."

Not really. I'd prefer to spend time with Detective Metz on some neutral ground, like a theater or a Hardee's. But I say okay. I normally like surprises.

Mavis

I'm here in the kitchen wiping down the counters, and tidyin up from supper when Dr. D walks in from work. I says, "Hey there, Dr. D, we done ate without you, but I'd be happy to heat you up a bowl of Brunswick stew and a piece of cornbread."

Dr. D looks plumb wore out. He says, "I'm running late tonight. I have a new bookkeeper and needed to go over some details with him. It took a lot longer than I imagined."

"You want the stew or not?"

"Has Mary Beth eaten?"

"I can't rightly say, but I imagine she has," I says, tryin to keep my lips tight on what all MB is up to tonight.

"Sure, I'll have some stew. Smells terrific."

"What you're smellin is the Bubba Burger I just cooked for Floyd, here."

"Of course you cooked for the dog." He leans down and scratches Floyd on his sweet little head.

"I heat him up a hamburger every Friday. He's as much TGIF as anybody else around here."

Dr. D laughs and tells me Floyd is just *bidin* his time before he takes over the house.

Dr. D is still wearin his office clothes, so I tell him to run his behind upstairs and change out of that monkey suit, and I'll get supper for him. When he gets back to the kitchen, his stew is hot from the microwave and sittin on the kitchen table with the cornbread and a glass of sweet tea. I set down at the table with him cuz I'd like to chat with him about somethin in particular.

"You know, Dr. D," I says. "Remember when I picked up them shirts at your house?"

Dr. D nods and wipes his mouth with his napkin and says, "Did I forget to thank you? You were a lifesaver."

"No, you thanked me all right, but that ain't what I'm gettin at. I was gonna say how I seen them dog pictures in your yard."

Dr. D nods, then shakes his head like it's a real shame that dog is gone. Or else he's sorry all them pictures is stuck all over his grass, trees and house.

"Your ex-wife found that dog yet?"

He's got a mouth fulla cornbread so shakes his head again.

"Looks like that ex of yours is fixin to stay in town awhile," I says.

Dr. D stops chewin while I'm talkin.

"How long are you plannin on stayin here at the Rapturous Rest? Looks like forever to me. Law, that ex of yours is really messin with your life." But what I'm thinkin is, *Looks like Mary Beth Green is messin with your life.*

"Yeah," he finally says. "Having Jeanine around has been pretty inconvenient, but if she wasn't being such a pain in the ass I wouldn't have a respectable reason for hanging around here as much as I do. I mean, it wouldn't kill me to stay here longer."

Dr. D carries his bowl to the sink, washes it out, and sets it on the rack. "By the way, where is Mary Beth? Her car is out there, but when I knocked on her door she didn't answer."

"Mary Beth went out with a friend," I says. "To a movie." I pull me out a cigarette and light up. About now I need me a cigarette somethin fierce. It's breakin the rules, smokin in the house, but seems like I ain't the only one breakin rules these days. Mary Beth and me need to have us that little chat about Floyd.

Dr. D picks up a dishtowel and starts drying off the dishes on the rack and stickin them in the cupboard.

"Nice," he says. "She does so much for others, it's good for her to get out. Who'd she go with?"

I ain't gonna lie about this, so I take a drag of my cigarette and says, "That detective man."

32

DETECTIVE METZ'S CASA

Mary Beth

Being at Detective Metz's house is strange. I give the front yard a once over and am disturbed to discover he's a statuary person. He's got a pair of concrete deer standing in his side yard: a full-size, seven-point buck and a corresponding doe. Then he's got a couple of squirrel statues and an eagle with spread wings perched on a tree stump. Looks like Snow White might make an appearance any second. His lawn looks freshly mowed.

"You must really love animals," I say.

"Not really. Why?"

"The statues."

"I saw them at one of those statuary places off the highway. Aren't they cool? I bought the two deer and the eagle, and they threw in the squirrels for free."

I nod and say, "Cool."

Detective Metz opens his front door. Immediately, a wonderful aroma drifts out.

"Did you cook?" I ask, shocked.

"I did," he says, more humbly than I would expect, as he gestures me into his home.

"It smells incredible! What did you make?" I'm pretty surprised Detective Metz would cook. I hope he didn't take the day off just to do this.

"Coq au vin."

"Coq au vin? I've always wanted to try that." It's true, I have. I'm all over anything chicken with gravy. This is more than enough to help me get over the trauma of seeing the bald eagle statue.

I may even have to brag to Terry that someone cooked a gourmet meal for me, too. See how he likes that. Then I remember Terry did make me some pretty delicious eggs this morning. That makes two gourmet meals from two different men in one day. I'm making myself uncomfortable thinking about it.

"I got it out of *The Joy of Cooking*."

Even more impressive. I don't own many cookbooks myself, except *Rachel Ray's 30-Minute GET REAL Meals* and a 1955 Junior League cookbook that I inherited from my grandmother.

Detective Metz has two black leather sectional sofas that fit together in a big right angle, making a V that opens towards the most humongous flat screen TV I have seen in my life. He's got some golf clubs in the corner and a stack of DVD's on the floor. He's got this framed poster from the movie *Rambo* next to the TV, a larger-than-life picture of Sylvester Stallone with a bandana tied around his head and one of those bullet belts across his chest, machine gun ready. There is also a dining table at one end of the room, and it's all set up with black placemats and napkins, silverware, and red square plates.

I plop myself down on the sectional.

"So did you find spinach, or did you not? I'm just curious."

"You want a drink?" asks Detective Metz.

"Got any tea?"

"I was thinking more of something to help us relax. I have wine and vodka."

Vodka is something I have never drunk. My mother's alcoholism pretty much killed any natural curiosity I may have had in the liquor department. I tell him wine will be fine.

He hands me a glass of wine and I think of roofies. I'm vigilant to remember to always watch people when they pour you a drink. Only, I've never had to watch out for Mavis or the girl at the Hardee's who pours the sweet tea.

He sits across from me on the other sofa and says, "Long day for me." He takes a sip of his wine, then lifts his iPod off the coffee table, pushes buttons, and places it on a dock with speakers. "You like Usher?"

I don't really keep up with current music. Besides listening to Linda Ronstadt and Perry Como, I like the oldies radio station. I tell him that Usher is fine by me, but I'm nervous. I've got this uneasy feeling we're on a stage, and Detective Metz knows all the lines and I know none.

I place my wine on the table and stand up, walking slowly around his living room, like there's something here I haven't seen yet.

"Fancy TV," I say. Then I walk over to the window and look out at his yard.

"Aren't you going to drink your wine?"

"I might have to save it for dinner. I haven't eaten much today."

"Then we'll have to remedy that," he says, setting down his glass. He goes to the kitchen. I hear some rustling, and he comes out carrying two plates and sets them on the coffee table. One plate has cheese and sausage slices arranged in a spiral; the other is piled with tortilla chips with a bowl of queso on the side.

I pick up a piece of cheese and sausage and bite into it. Then another. I eat about seven chips dipped in queso before I take the first sip of wine.

He says, "I'm a big believer in alcohol bringing people together."

I almost spit out my wine.

"Let me be clear," he says in his best official policeman mode, like he's teaching a D.A.R.E. program. "Alcohol can be dangerous if you're not careful, but for moderate people, like ourselves, Mary Beth, it can help us relax and have real conversations. Drop our inhibitions. You get to see the real person. The person behind the uniform, if that's who I am to you. And to me, you're the person with the dead friend, the person dying to get her hands on his journal. All this formality stands in the way of us being ourselves. But there's more to both of us. Wouldn't you say?"

I cram another piece of cheese in my mouth and nod my head.

"Wow, you're really hungry." He looks at his watch and says, "We could probably eat now."

"Can I help with anything?" I ask through a mouthful of cheese.

"No, you just sit right there and get comfortable," he says and pours more wine in my glass. He pours himself vodka and carries it to the kitchen. A few minutes later, he walks out with a steaming platter filled with chicken and mushrooms, smothered in sauce the color of chocolate. This is not my grandmother's chicken and gravy. He sets the platter on the table and returns to the kitchen. He reappears with bowls of warm red potatoes and bright green beans. I'm amazed. When Detective Metz was eating at the Salad Station, I surmised he was more of a Jell-O with marshmallows person. I can't believe he went to this much trouble for me.

He pulls a chair from the table and motions for me to sit, and he nudges my chair up to the table and unfurls my napkin, laying it across my lap. He serves my plate, then his, picks up his fork and says with a dazzling smile, "After you."

Dear Lord, I could get used to this kind of treatment. Seriously.

The meal is delicious. I may have to learn to cook someday because there's no way I could ever get Mavis to make coq au vin, unless there's a frozen variety at Sam's Club.

While we eat, we talk about Detective Metz's job, and all the interesting parts it entails. He also tells me the downside to the job, like crime scenes and how troubling it can be dealing with innocent people affected by crimes. Especially the kids, he says. I love how he seems so affected by the children. It's surprising, especially after all that stuff he said in the car about children whining and crying, but I guess it's different when he's on the job. I tell him that would kill me, too. Then I tell him about my grandmother and how she left me her house on Main because neither my father nor Marcelle wanted to live in Brightleaf, and she wanted to keep it in the family. I explain how I came up with the boarding house idea. I am really enjoying myself, talking with Detective Metz – Clark – and stuffing myself with chicken, mushrooms, and potatoes. We continue talking about our interests, your basic getting-to-know-you type conversation, including me telling him about the Share Group. Which finally leads to Ned. I tell him how I looked up yohimbe and how upset I was when I learned everything about it, but that didn't sound like Ned at all. But Clark just says you never know about people. That you can't rule anything out. Finally, I bring up the journal.

"So can't you see why that journal is so important to me?"

Detective Metz says, "I can see how you might think reading it will help you figure out how your friend died. But he was probably just a loser anyway."

"Huh?"

He sips his vodka and says, "No, no, no. I didn't mean he was a loser. I didn't mean to say that. You want the journal? I'll get it!"

Detective Metz seems really happy to give me the journal. I thought it would be much harder to make him produce it. He walks over to the shelf, where he placed it when we first arrived. He holds it out to me and says, "Don't get your fingerprints on it because I have to get it back in evidence tomorrow. If you touch it with your bare hands everyone will think you were the one who killed him. Then I'll have to book you!"

"*Killed* him? I thought you said he wasn't murdered." I grab the journal with my napkin.

"I *only* kiss and tell," he says taking another sip of his drink.

"What?"

"I mean I'll tell you everything if you kiss me."

He's giving me the goofiest look. Then it dawns on me that he's had about four vodkas, not including the glass of wine he drank when we first arrived. I've seen plenty of drunks in my life. I cannot be bothered by it. I have the journal in my hand and need to do some speed-reading, so I ignore him. But it is hard to ignore him because while I am reading Ned's journal, Detective Metz walks behind my chair. I can feel him standing there, so close that my spine gets that funky tickle. Then I feel his hands on my shoulders. He starts giving me a massage. It is extremely distracting. Even worrisome. I put down the journal and look up at him looming behind me.

He says, "Do you like what I'm doing?"

"I can't say I'm crazy about it."

He says, "Maybe I need to work on your arms more" and starts rubbing my arms.

I put down the notebook, stare at the table straight ahead of me and say, "Clark, could you please stop? I'm very appreciative for that wonderful dinner, and we've had a nice conversation, but you promised if I had dinner with you I could read Ned's journal."

"Seems like I gave you two things," he says. "Dinner and the journal. You might owe me one." Then he puts more pressure on my shoulders.

I stand up. "Do I need to go outside with Bambi's mom and dad to read this journal?" I motion to his yard art visible through the window.

His expression changes from smiling to sullen. "No," he says. "Just sit on my sofa and read it. I'll leave you alone." He walks off to a back room to sulk. Presently I hear a toilet flush.

"Thank you!" I sit down on the sofa, open my pocketbook, and pull out a pen and an old envelope for taking notes. I open the journal and begin reading, jotting down anything that looks important, but there isn't much to read. The notebook has about fifty pages, but only fifteen are filled. Still, it's interesting. When I'm finished, I pull my cell phone from my purse and see that I have two missed calls from Terry. I wonder if Mavis told him about my date. I decide not to call him back but just see him at the house later on tonight. Now, about those video games—I need to find out what Ned was playing at the time of his death. They seemed to have significance to Doyle. Video games seemed mighty important to Ned, too.

Detective Metz comes out of the back and wants to know if I'd like a cup of coffee. I jot down a few more notes without looking up and say, "Remember once I asked you about the games you found at Ned's house? Do you remember what he was playing at the time? And yes, I'd love a cup of coffee."

There is silence behind me. Finally he says, "Cream or sugar?" So I turn around to tell him three sugars, but when I face him it looks like he's got himself a t-shirt like Mavis's. The male version of the bikini bod shirt. Then I realize he's not wearing a shirt. And the bikini he's got on his lower half is real and has a tiger print.

He says, "We should stop beating around the bush, Ms. Green."

I'm not sure if I should run or laugh. I've never been in a room with a man dressed this way before. Alone. On the beach sometimes you see old men with big bellies wearing those weeny bikinis, but Detective Metz is neither old nor fat. In fact, he's as fit as a person can be, and has a really hairy stomach and chest. I'm pretty sure I should start to worry.

"Thanks again for dinner," I say, slowly standing and placing the journal on the table, "but...I did not mean to give you the wrong idea." I pick up my pocketbook and carefully hang it over my shoulder and start walking towards the door. "I promise that when I accepted your dinner invitation, I wasn't anticipating you showing me your underwear." I'm moving in slow motion like he's some type of a wild animal (a tiger comes to mind) who might attack if I move too fast. One sudden move...and bang!

185

"I'm sorry you're not having a good time," he says.

"It's not that I'm *not* having a good time." I smile and shake my head. "Actually, I'm just not comfortable at your house with you right now. This is not really what I imagined when you asked me out."

"What did you imagine?" he asks.

He probably does this with every woman he brings over. And they are all probably like, *Oh, Clark! You're sooo handsome! Get me drunk! I want a massage! Show me your tiger underpants!*

I start for the door again, but he gets between it and me. The tiger bikini bottom is way too close to my person, and I start feeling light-headed. I ask him what he thinks he is doing, an officer of the law and all. And he tells me that I know what we are doing and to quit acting like I was born yesterday. I just stand there for a few seconds, thinking. Finally I say, "I need to use the bathroom. Bad."

He gestures towards the hall where I heard the toilet flush a while ago.

I close the bathroom door behind me and lock it. There's not even any soap or a hand towel in here. They say men are the worst about washing their hands after doing their business. All I have to say is I hope Clark washed his hands before getting busy in the kitchen over our dinner. I lower the toilet lid, sit, and think about what to do next. I've got a drunk policeman dressed like Tarzan out there trying to have his way with me. While I'm thinking, I flush the toilet, wait a few seconds, turn on the sink, and make a little racket. I'm terrified of opening the door. I might have to sleep in here tonight. Not like this flimsy door could keep out anyone who really wanted to get in. Then again, this is not *The Shining*, and Detective Metz is not exactly an axe-wielding Jack Nicholson. I bet if I didn't come out all night I'd be safe. So I sit a while longer, and presently I look at my phone again. No new calls. It's ten o'clock. I'm reminded of how similar this situation is to when I was hiding from Terry in The Grocery Palace bathroom. I've got to quit hanging around in bathrooms so much.

It is 2 a.m. when my cab pulls up to the Rapturous Rest. I pay the driver and close the car door as quietly as possible. I tiptoe up the steps and pull out my key, but the door is already unlocked. It quietly swings open. As I move towards the stairs, I notice a beam of light shining out from under the kitchen door. Looks like no one even thought of shutting down the house properly tonight. Looks like a case of *when the cat's away.*

I push the kitchen door open. Mavis and Terry are sitting at the table drinking coffee and talking in hushed tones. They immediately stop talking and stare at me, like I'm some curfew-breaking teenager wielding a twelve-pack.

Mavis says, "Well, well, well. Look what the cat drug in."

Terry just looks at me. He takes a sip of his coffee. His expression is neutral, as if he is thinking about something boring, like paper clips.

"What are ya'll still doing up?" I ask.

Mavis says, "It ain't every day that you're out this late, Little Lady. So if you thank the two of us is doin somethin outta character then you best look in a mirror."

"You're waiting up for me? You shouldn't have."

"Baby, I had no choice. I tried to go to sleep, believe me. But I kept worrying about you out with that hotshot detective. So me and Floyd, we finally got up to get us a hot cup of buttermilk, and who did we run into? Doc. He couldn't sleep neither."

I look at Terry, but he will not meet my gaze. I can't imagine what he's thinking. But I can guess. I decide to tell them the story of my night. With details.

"After nodding off on Detective Metz's bathroom floor for a few hours, I woke up and decided to do a brave thing and crack the door. A lamp was shining in the living room, but the house was silent as concrete. So I gathered my purse and shoes and stepped over Detective Metz, who was passed out facedown on his living room floor."

I'm not telling Terry and Mavis this part: when I stepped over the

187

passed out Detective Metz I discovered the tiger underwear was a thong. I felt faint at the sight of his hairy butt. But I forced myself to keep quiet and stay moving.

From there I ran out of his house to a waiting cab. I apologize up and down to Mavis and Terry for not calling.

By now Terry looks relaxed. He believes me, which is a relief. He has this funny smile like I'm some kind of really ignorant girl.

"I don't get why you would go out with a guy you said *leers* at you," he says.

"I wanted to see Ned's journal, obviously."

"Come on!" says Terry. "You knew he wanted to be more than friends."

"Okay," I say, embarrassed. "I was the teensiest bit flattered. But the last thing I expected was to see him round the corner looking like a Zulu gigolo."

"I had a similar thing happen to me once, too," says Terry. "It was so frightening. A woman I knew surprised me by jumping out in this stretchy suit."

Mavis raises her eyebrows.

I shake my head and say, "I'm going to take a shower in the carriage house."

I feel like I need to scrub extra hard.

33

SWIMMING AWAY FROM SINS

August 15, 1990

Dear Diary,

I got baptized last Sunday. I've decided being a Baptist is not ghastly like my mother says. After church a bunch of people went to the Brightleaf swimming pool to be dunked, and I went with them. My grandmother thought it was the finest thing to happen in Brightleaf since Smitty's Grand Opening in 1973. I wore the Little Mermaid swimsuit under a long white robe. I am still boycotting the pool, but it goes to show that I would rather be seen by half the town of Brightleaf splashing around in a long white choir robe than in that terrible swimsuit. When the preacher dunked me, I thought of all the bad things I'd ever done like read Marcelle's private letters, smoke cigarettes, lie, and The Huey Incident. And one time I dumped out a whole bottle of milk of magnesia on the shelf at the Rite

Aid. I felt a little bit bad about those things. I swear on the Bible that I did not know Huey had a pet rat. By now he knows it wasn't his beloved Mrs. Frisbee. But nobody else (Mrs. Bussy, the principal, or Huey's friends) was quite sure if he actually pulled a rat head from his locker. Not even his own mother totally believed him. Now that I am all baptized and everything, I might tell Huey the truth, that the rat head wasn't a figment of his imagination. Maybe.

My father called today. He tells me I should probably stay with Grandmother for a while longer. Even start school here, at least until my mother straightens herself out. Grandmother is a teetotaler. Which sounds very religious. But this is a huge relief for a girl like me who needs regular things: someone to help her with homework, pick her up from tennis at 5:45 instead of 8:45, take her shopping for shoes and a dress without having cocktail hour in the Dillard's restroom first, and have a routine supper with nice conversation. A girl like me also wishes she would not be awakened in the middle of the night by a grown lady rambling about how the cat doesn't love her the way he used to. She wants ordinary. At least until she is 16....X

34

NED'S SECRET

Mary Beth

We're only as sick as our secrets. I don't know who said it first, but it's true. People keep all kinds of secrets, ranging from the sinister to the ridiculous. Pick up a newspaper, and you'll find stories about congressmen or celebrities caught doing something embarrassing and secretive. Secrets are kept so jobs and social standing won't be lost, relationships won't fall apart, the children won't find out, but most often, to keep out of jail.

Sometimes I look into the faces of the people who've had secrets exposed, like that man Bernie Madoff. Or the teacher at the private school who hosted drug parties for his students in his apartment at night, seducing the young girls to whom he taught Shakespeare and Melville each day. I saw that teacher's picture in the paper. I studied it, trying to identify the deviant in his eyes, first covering the left side of his face, then the right. They say the right side of the face shows a person's dominant state best because it's ruled by the left-brain. The left-brain being the analytical and logical side. So I guess if a person were stark-raving mad they'd have no objectivity. They'd have a craziness living in their right eye. Sometimes when I study a face, half of it looks like it's been eating of the knowledge of good and evil forever, but the other side is a blank canvas for an expression that is waiting to happen.

Studying that teacher's face, beyond the careful necktie and tailored blazer, beyond the dark, wavy hair, I also studied his mouth. Did it have a sinister curve or twist or whatever it is bad people do with their mouths? I saw nothing. Not in the eyes, not in the mouth. I decided he had a clear conscience, except for maybe a slight crease across the forehead. The forehead gave him away.

So did Ned have a dark side? I look at the smiling photo of him in the newspaper. It's hard to tell much from black and white newsprint, but your gut can tell you a lot if you listen.

35

IN MEMORIAM

"This Share Group is dedicated to Ned's memory."

Since none of us could be at Ned's funeral, I tried thinking of some kind of ceremony that would bring closure for us here. I opt for a symbolic candle theme. When I was growing up, the Christmas Eve candlelight services at the Presbyterian Church created a kind of magical mood, like an angel just might bust in through the wall behind the baptismal font, like the Incredible Hulk. For some reason, holding a lit candle in the dark makes people feel introspective and maybe even a little bit holy. So I've got this big pumpkin pie scented Yankee candle in a jar, lit and sitting on the coffee table in the center of the circle. The whole house smells like pumpkin pie. I think Ned would approve and really appreciate that this candle represents his life. I bought a pack of those white emergency candles and pass them around. Winslow, Vanessa, Terry, Eleanor, Mavis, Angus, Jimmy, Baby George, Phil, Chauncey, and I are present – pretty much the whole group, except Ned. The plan is to give each person in the circle a chance to share some personal experience he or she had with Ned when the mood strikes. It's my hope that we will all grow richer in our understanding of Ned and towards one another through this process. They say funerals are more for the living than the deceased. We need to say goodbye.

I turn off all the lights and pull the curtains to increase the drama. Ned's candle is the only light until Vanessa leans over, and lights her candle.

She says, "That Ned was a funny thing." When she smiles, the gold star on her tooth gleams. "On occasion, I'd go over to the carriage house to see if that child needed any cleaning done, but you'd be surprised to know there was never nothing much for me to do, except dust. And how that boy loved to collect dust! But his dishes, they was always clean. He never had a toilet bowl ring or nothing. And kept his trash picked up, he did. I clean for lots of single mens, and they keep all kinds of trash. They got beer cans, milk cartons, pizza boxes, tangled up with dirty underpants, t-shirts, and sneakers. They got mold growing in the toilet and tub. You'd think they never had a mama to teach them nothing. But not Ned. And another thing, the one time I went to hang up one of his shirts, I seen they was all hanging in his closet organized by color, his shirts were."

I try to picture Ned's tie-dyed shirts arranged by varying degrees of color.

Vanessa continues, "And he had framed pictures of his mama and daddy, right next to a picture of Bob Marley. Now that tickled me." She laughs. "But next to Bob Marley he had him a picture of him, and I mean Ned, shaking the hand of George Bush."

"The president?" asks Jimmy.

Vanessa nods. "It was a picture of Ned shaking hands with George W. Bush. When he was the president."

"He never told us about that," I say. "Did he?"

Winslow says, "Many people shook hands with George W. Bush but will never speak of it."

I say, "Vanessa, did he tell you why he was shaking hands with the president?"

Vanessa nods and says, "So I says to Ned, what you doing shaking hands with the president? And Ned, he says he kept a bunch of folks from getting blown up at a concert one time. Says there were some terrorists gonna kill everybody."

"Terrorists at a concert?" asks Terry.

"He said it was… lemme think." Vanessa rubs her chin. "I think he said it was some anti-hippie…terrorists…or something. And that was very strange to me, too. I never heard of nothing like that."

"Anti-hippie terrorists?" says Winslow. "What? A group of preppies hell-bent on wiping out flower children?"

Vanessa says, "He told me it was at a Fish concert. I remember that because it reminded me of the Long John Silvers I just ate, and it surprised me that somebody would name their band that. Kind of like naming a band Dog or Cat or Pig."

"Phish? Really?" says Winslow. "I'd love to hear that story. But I don't get why somebody would target them."

"I don't know, either. When he told me, I just nodded and went about my business," says Vanessa. "No offense to Ned or nothing, but some people I clean for says some strange stuff, so I've learned to go about my business and say, *Mm-hmmm*. But Ned, he was a sweet boy."

"Good as gold," says Mavis, leaning forward to light her candle. Mavis holds the candle under her chin. The way the light hits her face makes her look a lot like Willie Nelson. "He'd come over before the Wednesday supper sometimes with a white box full of that black lava he picked up at the Starvos. How I love me some black lava. He'd hand over the box and whisper in my ear, he'd say, 'You don't gotta share it, man.' A few times I kept it to myself and nibbled on it all week, but most times I'd set it out there on the table for the dessert. Bet ya'll didn't know that

195

about the black lava, did you?"

Eleanor looks perturbed. She says, "Yes, we knew Ned was the one who brought the baklava, but I doubt he gave it to you to dole out as you pleased. Are you making that up?"

"Don't be gettin your knickers in a knot over there, darlin. I never did see you eatin any of it."

"All right, ladies," I say. "Keep it sweet. Anything else you want to add, Mavis?"

Mavis says, "There's a lot to say, but I just wanted to say that part about the black lava. He was always just real nice. One time I seen him give Manchild two dollars."

Winslow reaches out to light his candle. He says, "I guess those of us who don't live at the Rapturous Rest never really knew Ned as well, outside of our little therapy group here, but I can say this about him: he was always interesting, if not entertaining, and could do some damn fine breakdancing."

"He was the master," says Chauncey, lighting his candle, too.

Terry gets his flame going next. He pushes back his glasses and says, "When I first came to the Share Group here, I gotta admit it was because of Mary Beth."

Everybody looks at me.

"I went home that first night thinking every one of you was crazy," says Terry. "Especially Ned. But I woke up the next morning feeling a little lighter. The honesty was refreshing. I guess that's the essence of Share Group. So here's to Ned." He holds his candle high.

Chauncey says, "Hear, hear," and holds up his candle to toast Ned with Terry. Doyle and Jimmy both light their candles and lift them. So do Angus, Phil, and Baby George. For a minute there I'm worried Baby George and Phil will start telling booger jokes again. Or Angus might throw up. He's done it before. But they're quiet. Eleanor is the last to light her candle. She holds it under her face, making her appear gaunter than ever.

She says, "Ned and I had a special relationship. I'll always remember him as the future father of my children…that I will never have." Then she bursts out crying. Mavis hands her a tissue and pats her on the back, but nobody knows what to say. Most of us are probably betting that the *special relationship* is all in Eleanor's head. To ease the discomfort in the room, I move on with the ceremony.

I have this little eulogy that I wrote and practiced into a tape recorder a couple times. I figure now is the time for it, so I gesture to the Yankee candle and say in my best funeral director tone, "This candle represents Ned's life on Earth, and now that we all have our candles lit by him, each of us enriched by his life in some way, I'm going to blow out Ned's, although his memory will burn in our hearts and minds forever. And as the pumpkin pie scent lingers in the air, so does the spirit of our dear friend." I stand and blow out Ned's candle. And in that I feel the loss of a presence in my life, a friendship truncated by some unknown force.

We sit for a few more minutes, our faces illuminated by the emergency candles, until I believe a respectable amount of time has transpired before our fingernails catch fire. I blow out my candle and sit in the dark for a few seconds. Everyone follows suit, and stillness settles into the room. I quietly rise and flick on the lights. Three or four people are crying into tissues. Others are hunched over, their hands over their eyes. We are all in some state of meditation or prayer for Ned, it seems.

When the ceremonial part is over, I plan to segue into part two of our meeting: the circumstances surrounding Ned's death. After another few minutes of reflection, I ask, "Anyone have anything else they'd like to say before we move on?"

Everyone looks at one another and shakes his or her head.

"Okay, then. I've got some things I'd like to share. I've been looking into this for the past few weeks, picking up odds and ends from the police, the library, Doyle, and even from Ned himself.

"I'm not a detective of course, but I think I know how Ned died."

The room is especially silent. Even Floyd notices and stops scratching. Several faces look worried.

Then two voices break the silence simultaneously: "I killed him!"

They stare at one another, Eleanor and Jimmy, like they are challenging one another as to who should get recognition for killing Ned. And it's like the whole room awakens to this new revelation, this new disclosure.

Eleanor screams, "I did it! I poisoned his spinach!" She starts to bawl. "I didn't mean to kill him! I just wanted him to get really sick, so I could nurse him back to health! So he'd need me! I put castor bean in the spanakopita I bought from Mr. Stavros and brought it up to Ned's apartment. I told him to accept it as a token for a long, successful life." She sobs into her hands, her whole body trembling.

Jimmy says, "I'd be happy to let Eleanor take all the credit for killing Ned. But I did a dumb thing. I gave him a drug most people are not familiar with called yohimbe. I can't help but wonder if that killed him, although I can't see how." Jimmy puts his face in his hands. Then he turns to Eleanor. "Where'd you get your castor bean?"

"Etsy.com."

"You gave him the yohimbe?" I say to Jimmy.

"How do you know anything about that?" Jimmy asks. "I know the police found it in his apartment because they asked me about it, but I stayed mum. It's not like it's illegal. I didn't want to implicate myself for nothing."

" For starters, he could have taken Viagra for his impotence," I say. "But you had to go and pretend to be a doctor and practice your mad scientist thing on him."

"Ned was impotent?" Jimmy and Eleanor ask, speaking in unison for the second time.

Eleanor's face smoothes into a smile; then she happily cries, "That explains so much! Oh, sweet Ned! I should have never killed you!"

Jimmy sits there looking at Eleanor, dumbfounded by what just came out of her mouth, like she's some kind of mutant. Like half woman, half Komodo dragon. Then he starts laughing. Jimmy points his finger at Eleanor, almost touching her nose, and laughs so hard his face turns purple. I can see all his teeth, and they are a lot whiter than I would have imagined. He finally chokes out, "Ned wasn't impotent, you evil bitch! Ned just had zero interest you. You knew that. He was only nice to you because Ned was nice to everybody."

Eleanor's face is blank with shock, but Jimmy keeps laughing. I'm worried he'll up and die from lack of air. Eleanor bursts out crying again.

Those two are a sight to behold, Jimmy laughing and Eleanor sobbing.

Finally, Jimmy catches his breathe and says, "I gave him the yohimbe for *hair growth*…for premature balding—and it was working too! I was keeping the dosage low, so I still can't see how he OD'd. I stressed to Ned the importance of following my instructions. I even advised him to quit drinking coffee and using any other recreational substances while I was treating him."

Hair loss? His hair looked perfectly fine to me. Some men are sensitive about those types of things, though. How tragic if he died because of it. At this revelation, things begin to settle down. Even Eleanor stops crying. Now it appears she's reverted back to being pleased she tried to poison Ned.

So Ned wasn't impotent. He was taking the drug for hair loss.

"Okay," I say. "I had that part wrong. But guess what else?"

No one can guess, so I remind them of Ned's dream about Evil Otto.

"Evil Otto, again?" says Terry.

I tell them I wanted to find out why Ned would dream about him so much. I do not tell them how I came to read Ned's journal and definitely skip the part about Detective Metz's tiger underpants. I tell them how I found out that he's the villain in a 1980's video game called *Berzerk*. I nod at Chauncey, who tried to tell us all this a few weeks back.

"That was a controversial game for a while," says Winslow. "When I was in grad school a guy did his thesis on the effect of video games on the developing mind called, *The Mind in the Machine,* and I vividly remember him telling me how several kids died of heart attacks after playing marathons of that game."

I say, "Evil Otto is just a smiley face, like Chauncey was saying a few weeks ago. But that makes him more terrifying."

"Big deal," says Baby George. "I watch scary shit all day, and I ain't dead."

I unfold a piece of paper and read, "According to an article by Cracked. com, entitled "The Ten Most Terrifying Video Game Enemies of All Time," Evil Otto was voted the scariest video game villain in the world." I read, "'It was Otto's job to fly through the poisonous walls and zap you when the timer ran low. Otto was merely a pain, but what makes him truly frightful is the fact that he is possibly the only video game enemy in history to kill players in real-life. Between 1981 and 1982, two teenage *Berzerk* players died of heart attacks shortly after posting high scores at video arcades. *Evil Otto watched them die...with a smile on his face.*'"

Mavis shudders.

Terry shakes his head and says, "That's sick."

"You think he was killed by the video game?" asks Jimmy.

"Maybe yohimbe and *Berzerk* together. I think he had a heart attack."

Jimmy's mouth falls open. He says, "I can buy that."

"Who would imagine that an herb for hair growth and a video game could create such a lethal combo," says Terry. "Weird how each of them could cause a cardiac arrest all on their own."

We sit there letting this soak in, and finally Jimmy says he should probably go to the police and tell them about the yohimbe.

Then Jimmy stops. "Wait a minute. What if it was Eleanor's castor bean that killed Ned?"

"He could be right about that," says Terry.

Winslow says, "Well, now we know why the police were treating Ned's death like a murder. They found spanakopita spiked with castor bean on his kitchen counter. Who would poison spanakopita? Some ruthless Greek grandma or somebody?"

I don't tell them that Detective Metz told me it was yohimbe, but the truth is, Ned could have had castor bean in his system, too. I recognize Detective Metz didn't tell me everything.

Vanessa says, "Castor bean. Sweet Jesus. I tell you who should go to the police, and that's Eleanor. She needs to be locked in the loony bin."

"Or locked in the bathroom, one," says Mavis.

"Bathroom?"

"She ran in there a minute ago when she was doin all that blubberin. We could trap her in there and call the police."

Eleanor *did* confess to a true crime. It also dawns on me that she maybe needed a little more than being told she was *all right*.

36

THE TRUTH HURTS

The next morning, Mavis walks into the kitchen carrying Floyd and a
bottle of peroxide. I'm sitting at the kitchen table reading the paper and
drinking one last cup of coffee before I leave to pick up the preschoolers.

"What are you doing?" I ask.

"Returning Floyd to his near-natural color," she says.

"But why?" I sip my coffee but accidentally take too big a gulp.

"So's his old owner will find him."

I choke, then cough so hard I have to hold my arms in the air.

"Catchin' cold? Hope you got the consumption," says Mavis, pursing
her lips.

"Mavis!"

She can't do this, not now.

I slowly say, "Mavis, you love Floyd. You can't hand him over to an
abusive perv–"

"Abusive pervert, my foot," says Mavis. "I'm givin him back to Dr.

D's ex-wife, and you know it, Miss Mary Beth Green. What you done was nasty. Not only to Dr. D but to poor Floyd here. And to think I called you a hero."

That last thing cuts me to the quick. There is nothing worse than someone who fakes being a hero. I lied, but didn't mean to pretend I did something valiant. I've never seen Mavis this angry, but I should have expected it.

"Mavis, please don't do this."

"Tough titty."

"Mavis, I'm so sorry I didn't tell you sooner. I'm really really sorry."

"Yeah, baby. Me, too," says Mavis. "Me and Floyd here was a team, we was partners, but the second I seen them signs Dr. D's ex stuck up all over town, I knew. And I know what it is to lose a child. I know what that woman feels now that Floyd's gone." She will not look at me.

"Mavis, I–"

"You let me down. I thought you was a little more holy than me, what with your scriptures hangin all around and the way you're so good to most folks. I was wrong."

I want to tell Mavis that no, she was not wrong. I *am* good. She didn't see how awful it was having the Jersey Guy behind me all those days. But seeing her anger combined with sadness tells me she's right. I am not good. I cannot bring myself to tell the truth or do the right thing concerning Floyd. I can't. I won't.

I finally say, "Mavis, I know this won't mean much to you, but I'm proud of you for doing the right thing, especially knowing how much you love Floyd. But I have a teensy request to make of you."

Mavis looks at me. Floyd is sitting in the sink, still blue, with water running over his curly coat.

"Could you at least give me a few more days? I should be the one to tell Terry that I flat-out stole his dog when we were still strangers. Then we can give Floyd back to Jeanine."

Terry might hate me, but at least Jeanine will leave him alone, and he can return to a normal life.

Mavis looks at me, thinking it over. Then I say, "For Floyd's sake."

She finally agrees. "For the sake of Floyd, here." She lifts Floyd out of the sink, wraps him in a towel, and carries him to her room.

37

THE PORT-O-LET

I wake up in the middle of the night, and dearly wish the plumbing was complete. I hate using the port-o-let at night. This whole process has turned into sadism on the part of the plumbers. I grab the pink robe and creep downstairs, quietly opening the side door.

The night air is clear and almost cool. Now I'm grateful I got up, to experience this quiet, purple night. I breathe in the fragrant air of the nearby tea olive tree and give myself over to the night noises: a solitary rushing car, a distant siren, and a boatload of crooning crickets. I make my way to the plastic blue cubical, peeking inside to make sure no person *or animal* is in there. I step in, lock the door, and sit down in the moonlit stall. I close my eyes and open them. I notice a tiny blinking. I close my eyes and open them a second time. There it is again, and it's coming from inside the port-o-let. I stand up, rearrange my robe, and step out, holding the door wide open so the streetlamp will shine in.

Then I see it; it's so small nobody would ever notice it during the day, but there it is, a little red light blinking every few seconds in something like an air freshener stuck to the wall. I instinctively understand what this means: I am being filmed. I snatch it off the wall and put it in my pocket, sickened, but not surprised. Perverts lurk everywhere. I'd turn this over to the police, but then Detective Metz and everyone would watch it, me being one of the stars of this port-o-potty production.

I suddenly feel like someone is watching me. I cannot run fast enough up the side steps. I keep feeling like a hand will grab me before I get there. When I reach the door, my hand is trembling so much it's hard to turn the handle. Then I hear a loud, *Clang! Clang! Clang! Clang!* It seems to go on forever. Either the house is falling down, or the person who planted the hidden camera is running towards me, full tilt, banging cymbals. Then silence. Floyd starts barking from Mavis's room. I stand still, unsure if I should stay inside or go out again. Which is safest? Then I hear footsteps, running. Running away, down the front path. I walk out to the yard, and when the footsteps reach the streetlamp, I clearly see Manchild. I just stand there, doing nothing, and watch Manchild pound down the street pushing an empty wheelbarrow, until he's completely out of sight. I tip-toe around to the front of the house, hardly believing my nerve, and up the front steps. Lights are already turning on throughout the house, and somebody hits the porch light. There on the porch, in front of the row of rocking chairs, is a king-sized pile of copper pipes. Enough to plumb a ten-room house. There's a piece of paper fluttering in the breeze on top of the pile. I hold it up to the light.

It reads: *marrybeth I'm a honest man now cents that preacher fixt me. sorry for yer troubles. manchild*

Mavis opens the door, and I hand her the note. She reads it and says, "What preacher? That rapscallion? The one that sent him to the hospital?"

I shrug and nod. Stranger things have happened.

38

DR. KELLY

"Looks like our next caller is Mary Beth from Brightleaf, North Carolina. Hello, Mary Beth! You're on the Dr. Kelly show!"

Here I am, lumping myself with all the morons in the universe by calling Dr. Kelly, but I could really use a pep talk. If Manchild can own up, so can I. And I know of no better individual to help me through this.

I say, "Hi, Dr. Kelly. This is Mary Beth. I'm actually calling for a girlfriend of mine."

Dr. Kelly says, "Why doesn't your friend call me herself?"

"Because she's embarrassed."

Dr. Kelly says for me to tell her what the problem is. So I say, "My friend thought this stranger was stalking her, so she stole his dog just to show him that two could play at that game."

Dr. Kelly says, "Dognapping is a felony. Your friend doesn't sound very intelligent."

How dare she?

I take a deep breath and say, "She's actually a smart lady but just got confused. She treats the dog very well but now has met the owner – the stranger she took it from – and has discovered he's a nice man. A very decent man–"

"First of all, your friend is dumb as a box of rocks," says Dr. Kelly. "No mature, intelligent person steals a dog to get even with a stranger. If you have a stalker, you call the cops. You don't stalk back. Okay? Secondly, I don't care how well she treats this dog. You must tell Cruella de Vil that the dog is not hers to keep. Thirdly, what were you going to say? That your friend wants to have a romantic relationship with a man she's *lying* to? What a great idea! Not!" Dr. Kelly is getting really worked up. "Healthy relationships are never built on *lies*. Tell your friend she needs to come clean and stop thinking she can get away with being such a creepy bandit!"

"Creepy bandit?"

"If the shoe fits!" says Dr. Kelly. "You can tell your friend *I* said so!" Then, in a perfectly calm tone, she asks, "Does that help you?"

"I guess," I say.

"Okay," says Dr. Kelly, "Our next caller is Myrna from Hilton Head. Myrna, you're on the *Dr. Kelly Show*!"

39

CONFESSIONAL

Terry is here, pestering me with that serious look again.

"Mary Beth? Will you go for a drive with me?"

Mavis expects me to tell him about Floyd. And Dr. Kelly was right: I can't build a relationship on lies. Ever since calling the show, I've been mustering up the nerve to tell Terry about Floyd and preparing for the worst. If he decides he doesn't want anything more to do with me, I'll deal with it.

It's not like I've got a shortage of suitors. Not that any of my suitors, other than Terry, are so hot. If I went on *The Dating Game* and picked bachelor number two, with my luck he'd turn out to be Pol Pot.

"All right," I say. "But it's got to be a quick drive. The plumbers may need my advice on something."

Terry starts the engine, and we drive slowly down Main Street, passing under a canopy of ancient elms, walnuts, and oaks. He turns off at Brightleaf City Park and pulls into an empty parking lot the size of a basketball court. A water fountain sits next to a big sign that details a map of the park and the hiking trail that leads to the river. The sign has a picture of a large golden tobacco leaf, a reminder that Brightleaf wouldn't be here had it not been for the booming tobacco industry.

Picnic tables sit unoccupied under shade trees, and a breeze pushes swings dangling from rusty chains. Most likely the very swings Marcelle and I played on as children. On weekday mornings, the park is deserted, except for a handful of joggers. But after the school bell rings, it gets packed with children, moms, and babysitters. Today, a lone man jogs the perimeter of the soccer field to the left.

Terry unbuckles his seatbelt and turns toward me. He takes off his glasses, which gets on my nerves because now his eyes look itty bitty and half blind. Since I'm probably all blurry now, I can't even roll my eyes because he won't see it. I go ahead and unbuckle my seatbelt and face him, acknowledging that I recognize he's in a serious kind of mood. I might-should even be scared.

Terry is sweating for some reason. He swallows and says, "Mary Beth, I've been honest about my life and hobbies at the risk of looking ridiculous to you…"

"I had to follow you to the Trekkie convention."

He holds up a hand, nodding. Then he loosens his tie and says, "I wanted to invite you but didn't know you well enough. I wanted you to like me for myself, the way I like you for yourself, quirks and everything." He starts messing with the Swiss Army knife on his key chain. Flips out the bottle opener and shuts it. Then looks at me and says, "I need you to be honest with me."

My fingernails are uneven, and I'd give anything for an emery board right now. I glance at Terry. He looks at me with a stony silence. Just come right out and ask: Did I steal Champagne, the pink stuff, Floyd?

"So I'm just going to come right out and ask you something—aware I might be risking our friendship," says Terry.

210

I feel like screaming, *Just do it!*

"Mary Beth, will you marry me?"

I hear it, but my mouth is already open, and my vocal chords have already been given clearance, and it's just too bad for me that I end up shouting, "Yes! I stole your dog! And dyed him black!"

He looks at me without his glasses. He is silent.

Then he grabs my face with both hands and he kisses me on the mouth. He kisses me so hard I feel like he's trying to kill me for all my badness. It doesn't hurt, but I start crying anyway. Terry must think I'm silly for crying, but he keeps kissing me even when my tears roll between our lips. I'm definitely kissing him back, even though the gearshift is right between us, like somebody placed it there on purpose to prevent people from making out while sailing down the highway at eighty-five. Gearshift/console notwithstanding, Terry is holding on to me like any second I might go flying out the window. Now he's squeezing my back, up and down my back, and oh, Lord, under my shirt. He's kissing my eyelids, cheeks, and neck murmuring, "Mary Beth...I love you. I've loved you since you told me you lived in the urology clinic and ate chili out of bedpans."

I can't help but laugh. I wipe my tears with my sleeve. First I cry like a child, now I laugh like a drunk. I take a deep breath and retrieve my composure, but I think that I probably knew all that time, too. Why? Because when I first opened my eyes after sleeping in his office and looked right into his face, I thought I was still dreaming. I thought, *Here he is. The person I've been waiting for all this time, and he is going to kiss me.* But then I realized he was only my doctor. Then I realized it was the Jersey Guy, and that really burned my biscuits. But he was nice and calm, intelligent and friendly. And yes, he is a fine-looking man. And maybe it was because I felt so vulnerable at the time. He caught me in the curious combination of being both asleep and half-naked. And I trusted him. On the spot, I developed an involuntary crush on him the size of The Forbidden City, right there in his office. Yes, the Jersey Guy. One day I was hoping for him to die really quick; the next day I was inviting him to my home.

I forced him out of my mind, decided that lots of ladies probably get a crush on their doctors. And how stupid it is to take one look at a man and suddenly be *in love*. Anyway, Mary Beth Green does not foster crushes. She does not let her heart out of its crypt, much less out on her sleeve. And my heart would still be dead and buried if it were not for the honesty of this man. Honesty is what I love the most about him. Probably because it is something I suck at sometimes.

I'm trying to decide which base he's gotten to. Does unfastening my bra count as second base? I hope that jogger can't see us because it seems Terry might be inclining toward third base or even hitting a home run, based on the way he's clutching me. He will not let go, like he's drinking water for the first time after eating sand or fire. And I feel the same way, like a person who's never been held in her whole life. And I never have. I feel like shouting, "Take me!" And I think of my grandmother, standing there next to the Lord in Heaven. And she's arguing with the Lord, begging, "Can't you stop them?" and the Lord saying something about Free Will.

Terry kisses my neck and unbuttons my shirt, right there in the City Park, in his Lexus. I guess it's not enough to feel my breasts, but he's got to take a look at them, too. He's not wearing his glasses, so I'm not as embarrassed as I should be. No man has ever laid eyes on my naked breasts before, but then I remember Terry is a gynecologist, and he's looked at zillions of breasts. Then I worry that he might be comparing me to all those other women, so I block that thought and think of my grandmother still standing there with her mouth hung open, and I say to her in my head, "Grandmother, you don't need to watch this very un-Baptist moment, so you might as well cover your eyes. I want him to take me! To hit a home run right here in this Lexus." Then I say it out loud, "I want him to take me all the way home."

"What?" Terry pulls back. He's breathing hard, and his face is flushed.

I give him my sexiest look, which I forgot he can't see without his glasses, and whisper, "Take me home."

He pauses, takes a deep breath, and says, "I'm sorry. I didn't mean to, I mean…Okay, I'll take you home."

Wait. What just happened?

"No! Don't take me home!"

But he's picked up his glasses and is wiping them off already and setting them back on his face. And I don't know how I ruined one of the best moments of my life. A man just told me he loves me, and not just any man. I told him I stole his dog, and he kissed me. We were making out! How did it all end so quickly?

He thinks I'm a slut.

"Terry?" Clicking my seatbelt in place and trying to fix my hair, I say, "I'm not normally like that, you know – fast. Just know that I'm not the way I seemed." My goodness, my heart is still pounding from all that interaction. I'm embarrassed, too, because I really was all set to give it up right there in the parking lot, in front of joggers, school children, janitors, hobos, anyone who may pass. "Do you think bad of me?"

Terry shakes his head. "You said you wanted me to take you home."

"Oh."

When he pulls up to the curb in front of my house, I jump out before he does and walk around to the driver's door. Terry rolls down his window. I take a deep breath and say, "We should do that again sometime."

"Good," he tries to say with a straight face. "Now, give Jeanine her dog back." And he's smiling.

Oh, *Redbook*. Eat your heart out.

213

40

THE NEXT DAY

"Well, I told him," I say to Mavis.

"About Floyd?" Mavis looks sadder than I've ever seen her. She's in the kitchen making pigs in blankets, hotdogs rolled up in Hungry Jacks.

I nod.

"How'd Doc take it?"

Her t-shirt says, *What Happens In The Graveyard, STAYS In The Graveyard.* I feel like I should be reassured by this message, but somehow her shirt makes her more tragic.

"He should be by in a minute to talk to you about it," I say.

"That's good," she says without emotion, smashing the dough flat.

I stand there watching her pound out pre-made dough and chop hotdogs in silence until we both hear the front door open and shut. Then we hear all kinds of clattering going on in the living room on the hardwood floors.

"Who the hell is making all that racket?" Mavis wipes her hands on her apron and punches open the kitchen door.

Floyd comes running through in all his blueness with a snowball white puppy scampering behind. Floyd comes to a sudden halt, and the puppy pounces on him.

For the first time in days, Mavis smiles and says, "Who's your friend here, Floyd? She's a purty little thang." She kneels down, scoops up the puppy, and rubs its head. "Hey there, darlin. Ain't you cute." The puppy is a ball of energy and cranes its neck to chew on Mavis's hand.

Terry stands with his arms crossed, looking especially fetching today. I haven't told anyone about Terry's proposal. I hardly believe it myself. We'd probably shock the pants off everyone because they barely saw us going out together. We didn't. But good Lord, how my heartbeat picks up just looking at that man. I must avert my eyes.

"Do you like her?" asks Terry, motioning to the puppy.

Mavis smiles and says, "Who wouldn't like a puppy?" She pulls the puppy close to her face and rubs her nose on its ear. The puppy licks Mavis's cheek and mouth, hovering like a hummingbird over her face. She laughs and wipes her mouth with her sleeve. "You rascal," she says and gives the puppy a squeeze.

Terry sticks his hands in his pockets and says, "She's yours…if you want her." He gives Mavis an uncertain look like he's attempting a trade and hoping she'll accept.

Mavis strokes the puppy but sets it down and says, "Ain't no need. I 'preciate the gesture. It's cute and all, but it ain't Floyd."

Floyd and the puppy set off, tearing all over the downstairs again, tumbling over one another.

"No dog could ever fill Floyd's shoes, dog-wise, but maybe a puppy could help make things a little better," I say.

Mavis purses her lips and shakes her head, turning towards her room. I admire Mavis for being the person who insisted on doing the right thing, giving Floyd back to his rightful owner. She loves him more than any of us. Except for Jeanine, that is.

"Hello, hello!" A voice rings through the house.

"Hello?" I say, looking at Terry, shrugging. I call, "We're back here."

We hear a clicking of shoes across the wood floor until she comes into view.

"Jeanine!" Terry says. "What are you doing here?"

Speak of the devil. Jeanine is a small, tightly built woman, with short, dark glossy hair, and the greenest eyes I've seen in a while.

I say, "Jeanine?"

Terry says, "I apologize for not introducing you before now. Mary Beth, Mavis, this is Jeanine, my ex-wife."

I'm not really sure what to say. What do you say to a person who you know all about, but they know nothing about you?

"We've heard so many good things about you!"

"Well, thanks," she says.

"He tells us you're a wonderful cook," I add, ever so thankful that I thought of one of Jeanine's virtues. For a few seconds, the only thing I can picture is Jeanine making coffee wearing lingerie. "Terry tells us that you make the best scallop lasagna in the world, and I'm so jealous because I can hardly boil water."

Terry says, "Jeanine is on a break from the Navy. She just came back for a brief period to find her dog."

This is new.

"You didn't tell us Jeanine's in the Navy. That's terrific," I say.

It's bewildering to have Jeanine standing in my kitchen, in the flesh. In my mind, she'd almost started taking on folklore status. She was fast becoming *The Legend of Jeanine*. Here I was imagining Jeanine some big socialite and that she left Terry to go jet-setting with a European tycoon, and all along she's been a military woman. It's weird that Jeanine isn't the glamorous lady I imagined. I mean she's in good shape and pretty and

216

all but just not the celebrity look-a-like I imagined, like Heidi Klum or Gwyneth Paltrow.

If Terry hadn't been here to identify her, I'd think she was a realtor. Realtors are always coming by, telling me how they'd love to sell this house.

Terry says, "Will you guys excuse us for a minute?" He turns towards Jeanine and guides her a few paces away. "So what's up?"

"You mean, what took me so long to find you?" She sounds exasperated.

"My cell is on. I haven't been hiding from you, if that's what you mean," says Terry.

Seeing Jeanine makes me feel like she's someone I should have met before. And so should Mavis and Winslow and Jimmy, and everyone else. But then I think of Floyd. And think I'd let her sleep in the street before I'd let her take Floyd from Mavis.

And that's when I hear the patter of dog paws approaching. I realize it's too late to think those kinds of thoughts anymore.

Floyd stops cold.

The puppy is feverishly using one of Floyd's legs as a chew toy, but Floyd stands stock still, staring at Jeanine.

This is the moment I've been dreading for weeks. I know Jeanine will know her dog, the way Mavis says. Mavis says you can look your dog in the eye and know it, no matter what color.

Jeanine notices the dogs and freezes. We all freeze.

Floyd stares at Jeanine and Jeanine stares back.

This is one of those times when you hold your breath. The situation has finally reached a tipping point. And then something odd happens.

Time seems to slow down. A peace settles over me. The light and colors of the room shift. Jeanine, Terry, and Mavis recede in my vision and the room fades to another moment in time: My mother standing right where Jeanine is standing, coming to drag me back to Atlanta with her for my senior year in high school. And Mazie putting her foot down and defying my mother to take me away. To pull me from this place, this house where I learned to play bridge and crochet; where I listened to old records and had slumber parties. Things other kids would call old fashioned I called safe. I was safe. All thanks to Mazie Lee Green.

The voice of Jeanine breaks my trance: "What cute dogs! They are so adorable! And would you just look at that…"

Look at what? What does she want us to see? How much the bigger blue dog, which obviously recognizes her, favors Champagne? The very dog she's been searching for is right here on Main Street. Is that what she wants us to see? I can't look. Terry is just as upset as me, but Mavis is resigned, despondent. Past being sad. Mavis just is.

Jeanine says, "You can tell they love one another so much. Is that a mama and her baby?"

No one answers her. The puppy takes a break from accosting Floyd and pees on the floor. Floyd is still staring at Jeanine.

Jeanine bends her knees, holds out her hand, and says, "Hey there, sweet puppies. Come see me!" She smiles her biggest, expecting the dogs to come towards her.

Floyd becomes unfrozen and starts walking towards Mavis with his tail between his legs. The puppy is unfazed and sticks to Floyd like a tick. Mavis bends down to gather Floyd, and he stands on his hind legs and pushes his way into her arms.

"Well, look at that," says Jeanine. "The mama dog loves *her* mama!"

I'm dumbfounded. Jeanine needs glasses. Floyd is obviously a male dog with a penis. But Jeanine only sees a big dog and a little dog and translates it mother and baby.

It's clear that the choice was Floyd's. He chose Mavis. Floyd the dog is no fool. He knows not only the hand who feeds him but the one who loves him best. That's how I see it.

At this moment, I lose all guilt. I feel like if I handed Jeanine a billy goat and said, "We found Champagne," she'd put it on a leash and proudly walk it around the block. She might even enter the billy goat in a poodle competition.

I am a free woman.

Mavis nods and says, "You a good girl, ain't you, Floyd?"

Terry says, "Whatcha need, Jeanine? Laundry detergent or something?"

"I came by to give you the keys," she says, jangling the keys to his house. "As much as I've loved every millisecond of Old Home Week, I need to get going. If my dog returns, call me ASAP, pretty please." Jeanine bats her eyelashes at Terry, but I look up at the ceiling so that he doesn't see me seeing it.

Looks like we've got two dogs now.

41

THE NED WRAP-UP

Detective Metz calls the house the next day. He is talking all official and calling me Ms. Green and thanking me for handing Eleanor over to him. Basically acting like the scene he made at his house didn't happen, and that's fine by me because this is the way I like it: by the book and professional. He tells me Eleanor is being evaluated by the court-appointed psychiatrist and that Jimmy will have to do forty hours of community service for not cooperating with an investigation, but I already knew all that because Jimmy told me.

Then he says, "For the record, you were right, Ms. Green. Mr. Hillman's cause of death was cardiac arrest. We checked his video game console and found *Berzerk*. We also conferred with Mr. James Riddle about the dosage of yohimbe he was taking. The yohimbe alone wasn't enough to kill Mr. Hillman. Looks like he never touched the spanakopita."

Which is good because if castor bean killed Ned, that would make

Eleanor a murderer. "Thanks for letting me know," I say. "I still want your recipe for coq au vin. I admit I can't stop thinking about it."

Detective Metz pauses then says, "I bought it at The Gourmet Gourmand. They'll sell you one with two sides for twenty dollars."

42

DOUBLE FINESSE

August 27, 1990

Dear Diary,

Last Wednesday at the soup kitchen, I cooked my first dish, a broccoli and cheese casserole. It was a gigantic hit with the foodless (Harriet told me to stop calling all of them homeless). Grandmother has also been dragging me around to deliver Meals-On-Wheels. I swan, that woman never stops. "I swan" is my grandmother's saying and my new saying. It's old fashioned, but I've been using it a lot lately when I play bridge with the old ladies, which is getting to be pretty dang fun, except for the dummy hand part. I am all signed up for school. I am not crazy about not going home and not seeing my friends for a while. It's depressing to start the 8th grade with no friends (and even more depressing to know all the Lawrence Welk dancers by name). But my mother isn't home, Marcelle is at college, and Daddy hasn't lived at home in years. There would be nobody there to help me celebrate my 13th birthday next month. Brightleaf isn't actually so boring anymore. I talked to one of the cigarette girls the other day. She told me they all quit, cold turkey. Come to find out they were in the 6th grade like I thought. I almost wrote Huey a letter telling him he really did see a rat head that day, but I might put it off for a few more years, after the statute of limitations runs out or something. I feel I owe it to him. Still, sometimes when I'm in my bed in the blue room, I think about Huey holding that package, sealed with the lipstick kiss, and wonder what he was thinking right before he opened it. I can't help but start laughing all over again....X

43

THE ANTI-HIPPIE FACTION

I wrote a letter to Ned's mother, telling her all the wonderful things about her son I never had the opportunity to say face-to-face. I included the clippings from the Brightleaf paper on his death, something I deliberated doing, but in the end decided she might want them. A week later, I get this letter from her:

Dear Mary Beth,

Your letter meant so much to my husband and me. Swallowing the fact that Ned is gone seems impossible, but to hear that others loved him as much as we did is a comfort. You mentioned Ned's athletic abilities, particularly his breakdancing. We are aware of his talents, especially since he's been active in the sport since high school and was part of a dance team which toured the nation. It was thoughtful of you to include the newspaper clippings from your local paper. It's sad reading them, but they are an important part of Ned's memory. You mentioned the photograph with George W. Bush—I've included a newspaper article with the story behind the photo. Another reason we were proud of our son. Thank you again for your love and concern. We hope to meet you next time we pass through Brightleaf.

Sincerely,
    Elizabeth Hillman

I unfold the newspaper clipping.

BOMB PLOT FOILED BLOCKS FROM THE WHITE HOUSE

DECEMBER 17, 2003, WASHINGTON, D.C.— *A stir was caused at MCI Center during a concert by the band Phish when police attention was drawn to a group of conservatively dressed women who have come to be known as the Bradley Bombers, named after the Vera Bradley bags they carry filled with explosives. A lone man noticed them and alerted security.*
"They just weren't cool, man," said Ned Hillman, the person responsible for notifying security. "Here it is, right after nine-eleven and you've got this group of uptight women pushing their way to the front with these preppy backpacks. Those moms were totally sending out a ton of negative energy."
When the women were confronted by MCI Center security and their backpacks searched, they confessed to being part of an anti-hippie faction with their spokeswoman saying, "The greatest problem with our nation is the visionless youth proliferated by the hippie attitudes of 1960's America, whose values continue to erode our society. If our deaths prevent future doctors and lawyers from getting derailed by drug addiction and a slovenly lifestyle, causing them to become pizza

deliverers and live with their parents until they're 50 years old, then we will have saved our country."

I remember this story. Everyone remembers it. And I remember the women saying that they didn't like being called the Bradley Bombers. They referred to themselves as the Victims. Ned never said anything about any of this to us. He saved all those people, and just a few blocks from the White House. And it actually says "anti-hippie faction."

There's a hand-written comment on the bottom of the story by Ned's mom:

FYI: The Brightleaf police had this information and originally thought Ned's death was in retaliation from this group. The FBI got involved.

Detective Metz knew all this. I'm starting to doubt the dream journal was even a part of the *official evidence*. I'm positive he knew about the castor bean spanakopita from the get-go. The fact that he totally made me think he was letting me in on top-secret police business makes me feel really dumb. Dumb as a box of rocks.

It's the end of another Share Group. I fold up the newspaper article with the letter from Ned's mother. Everyone was pretty fascinated by it all, especially the part about the FBI being called to Brightleaf to investigate. Meanwhile, Ned is probably up in heaven, breakdancing and keeping it real, oblivious to all the hullaballoo that's going on down here surrounding his death. Terry, Winslow, and Jimmy start pushing the furniture back into place and setting the folding chairs in the hall closet. Normally Eleanor would be here. She'd be rushing around, making sure everything was exact, all the knick-knacks and photographs repositioned on the coffee table, the wing chairs in their exact spots. I miss her some. She wasn't all bad.

Winslow says, "Hey, Doc, feel good having your own house back again?"

Terry says, "It feels good, but there's no place like the Rapturous Rest."

When Terry finally moved back to his house after Jeanine was packed and gone, he found all his boxer shorts ironed and hanging in the closet with his shirts. Also, his shoes were shined and his fridge sparkling clean. Jeanine made several scallop lasagnas and left them in the freezer with a note saying, *These are so you won't starve fending for yourself.* He brings them over to Share Group and tells Mavis he likes her lasagnas better, even though they're Stouffer's. The notion that Jeanine thought he would be helpless once she left makes me wonder—it's as if Jeanine imagined Terry being all alone, eating her lasagnas, like some old widower, sadly chewing and digesting the last morsels of his wife's existence. Even if Jeanine is a little cracked, I have to admit that those lasagnas are first-rate. And hopefully castor bean-free. Nobody's died yet.

"Don't you think it's strange that she thinks you're so needy?" I say to Terry.

"I am needy," he says. And he leans in to kiss me.

EPILOGUE

MAVIS BEAMS US THE HELL OUTTA HERE!

First off, I'm gonna say I ain't jealous of nobody goin on a cruise. Havin my two feet planted here on dry land is plenty adventure for a girl my age with two rascally dogs to look after. Lord, Mr. Sulu already done chewed up two pairs of Mary Beth's shoes and one of my sneakers. Top that off, he gnawed a hole clear through one of the sofa cushions. I keep tellin Floyd he needs to be a leader, show Mr. Sulu the way gentlemen dogs is s'posed to behave. Floyd, he just stands there watchin Mr. Sulu commit one crime after the next.

Doc and MB ain't no help, neither. Them two got hitched last Saturday at the Wendy's church. The whole Share Group was there, some of Dr. D's doctor friends, and so was Marcelle and her mama and daddy. I was the Matron of Honor, and honey, the Goodwill ain't never gettin that dress back again! MB told me I could pick out whatever I wanted, so I did, and baby, it's the one I'm gettin buried in. But that ain't nothin. You shoulda seen the bride and groom walk up to the Wendy's counter, where the preacher was standin, in them *Star Trek* leotards. When it came time for the rings, I whistled for Floyd, and he scampered up to Dr. D, fur on his head all slicked back like Elvis, and lets him pull the ring outta a little pocket on a bowtie collar we got for the occasion. My Floyd, a ring bearer! Now they're off on a *Star Trek* Celebrity cruise. I think Doc and Mary Beth is gonna be happy together. They're movin out to the carriage house when they get back, so MB can still run the Rapturous Rest, but so's they can have some privacy, too.

I know what you're wonderin. What ever happened to that Cruise for Three that Mary Beth was promised way back? Mary Beth changed her mind about lettin the Share Group draw straws; instead she turned it into a raffle. You could buy as many tickets as you wanted for fifty cent apiece. She donated the money to the soup kitchen. Anyway, Baby George, he probably bought near to seventy-five tickets, and he won all right. He picked Jimmy and Phil to go on the cruise with him. And we was all wonderin why he'd pick them two bozos instead of some ladies or somethin.

Baby George says, "We're a team, and we stick together! Plus, if I go on a cruise without them, Jimmy will fire me."

"True," says Jimmy.

Don't ask me about Eleanor or Manchild. I expect one's in jail and one's workin with the Salvation Army. Which is doin which? I do not know. Ain't it funny how life is?

Speakin of funny. We got us a new boarder. His name is Newman, and he's sweet on old Mavis, here. He's my age, about six feet tall, and skinny as a broken pencil. I could tell he took a shine to me when he'd creep out to the front porch and offer me cigarettes and Krispy Kremes all shy-like. Anyway, he's invited me out for Bingo two or three times, over to the old Harlan Hotel downtown. Somebody turned it into a senior center a few years back. So if you're ever lookin for the old folks of Brightleaf you'll find them all *up in* the Harlan Hotel. I mean they're packed in there and lovin every minute of it. But last time he invited me to Bingo, I drew

229

the line. I says, "Newman, if you want me to be your girl, you've got to think of somethin more interestin for us to do than sit around and play Bingo till we croak."

Newman may be shy, but he ain't stupid. Right off, he started plannin excursions for us. Since neither of us owns a car, we always take the Greyhound. So far we've been to High Point to see The World's Largest Chest of Drawers and Winston-Salem to visit The Giant Salem Coffee Pot (which I don't recommend because it ain't as giant as I hoped). Next we've got us an all-day field trip comin up. We're takin the bus to the Pamlico Sound to see the Belhaven Memorial Museum! It's a of museum packed full of shit somebody hauled out of this dead crazy lady's house, like a two-headed kitten, several mummified squirrels, and a dress worn by a seven hundred pound woman. I caint wait! But best of all, it's got a flea bride and groom that you get to look at through a magnifyin glass. And Newman thought this up just for me.

35095195R00143

Made in the USA
Charleston, SC
27 October 2014